M

of

Love

Dianna Nicolai

To Karen,
May the Lord bless you!
with much love
your cousin
Dianna

PublishAmerica
Baltimore

First printing

Hardcover 978-1-4560-1186-4
Softcover 978-1-4560-1187-1
PUBLISHED BY PUBLISHAMERICA, LLLP
www.publishamerica.com
Baltimore

Printed in the United States of America

In memory of my mother, Stella Wyatt
Also my good friend and mentor, Arlene Shelton

Goodbyes are not forever.
Goodbyes are not the end.
They simply mean I'll miss you
Until we meet again!

My sincere thanks to:

Julie Lee—for her idea for this story and her editing, but mostly for being an encouraging and supportive sister.
Kathy Morris—my other great sister for her encouragement.
Kellie DeHoet—daughter-in-law extraordinaire who graciously took time from her vacation to edit this book.
Craig DeHoet—a wonderful son and book promotion advisor.
Josie Higley—the most loving stepdaughter a woman could have and an awesome book promoter.
Cathy Gettman—super assistant, editor and confidant.
Hazel Smith—my cheering squad, one who always gives me the confidence to keep writing.
Pastor Jim Shelton—for leading me to the Lord and teaching me how to live for Him.
The Alpha Writers and Night Writers groups—who do such a great job of critiquing.

CHAPTER 1

Jill noticed the skis propped up against the back of the cabin the first time she went out to get wood for the fireplace. Now she stood looking at them, debating whether to try it.

A million diamonds sparkled off the freshly fallen snow as the morning sun gleamed over woods silent except for a few twittering birds. Enough of the powdery white had descended during the night to make the desire to fly down the mountain slope impossible to ignore. Common sense told her it wasn't wise to go alone. But maybe it was time to do something just for the sheer thrill of it. She'd been sensible all of her life.

She walked part way down the hillside, making sure the area was clear of fallen logs and other debris that could cause problems. Thoughts of the many times she and Tom went skiing entered her mind, but were quickly dashed. There was no point in dwelling on the past. Now she needed to make some changes in her life. The thought was scary, especially since she could no longer rely on God to help her. He let her husband die and left her alone to raise a three-year-old son. She wasn't sure she could trust a God like that.

Losing her husband in an auto accident a year ago was bad enough, but having another woman with him when he died was still almost more than Jill could bear. Thinking about Tom brought more sad memories. Just recently she found out her beloved father was not the man she thought he was either. He cheated on her mother, leading a separate life that no one knew about until after his death. The cabin Jill was staying in was her father's secret hideaway, one she hoped to dispose of quickly and return to her life in the city.

Men! They couldn't be trusted, so she would have to learn to do things herself. This looked like a good start. She put on the skis and pushed herself to the edge of the steep slope. The air smelled of pine. Trees below grew close together revealing only a narrow twisting path that soon was no longer in sight.

"Here goes," she proclaimed to no one. Jill's arms pushed downward and back on the ski poles with enough force to send her over the edge. The slope was steeper than she anticipated. Her speed increased. She veered right, then left, narrowly missing a giant pine tree.

Suddenly her right leg felt the jar of a ski coming in contact with something immovable. Her body plunged forward in midair, twisting and turning. Searing pain engulfed Jill when she landed on her right leg. She fought for control over the black waves threatening unconsciousness.

Jill forced her eyes open to look at her leg lying twisted in an unnatural position. *Now how am I going to get out of here?* Panic began to set in. *Stay calm. You have to keep a clear head and think this through.*

The sun disappeared behind thick gray clouds. Snow so thick she couldn't see through it began to fall. The faint breeze, barely noticeable earlier, turned into a full-blown wind. The long, wailing cry of a wolf sounded nearby.

"I am not going to die. I am not going to die," Jill repeated out loud, hoping to convince herself. She looked around for some type of shelter from the worsening storm.

Attempting to ignore the pain shooting up her leg, she pushed herself to a sitting position and removed the skis still attached to her feet. Waves of dizziness overwhelmed her and nausea threatened to relieve her of the breakfast eaten earlier, as she dragged herself to the base of a large leafless oak tree.

With mitten-covered hands, she swept snow over her body, covering it with the only substance she could find to use for warmth. Exhausted she leaned back against the tree's trunk. *Why did I leave my cell phone in the cabin? I'll just rest a little while. When the storm lets up I'll make my way back to the cabin. It can't be too far.*

~~~~~~~~

She was being lifted up. Tom was there to rescue her. She snuggled closer to the warmth of the body holding her close. A smile curved her lips, her eyelids slowly raised. But the eyes she met were not Tom's. Instead, the cold, steel-blue eyes of a stranger met hers.

A quick assessment verified Jill's suspicion. There was little doubt this was one of the mountain men about whom Jill had been warned. Choosing to stay alone at the cabin might not have been such a good idea after all.

Long blonde hair fell from beneath his coonskin cap. A thick, bushy beard, the same golden color as his hair, covered the majority of his face. Piercing eyes glared at her.

"What are you doing up here?" he growled.
~~~~~~~~

"I…I…was skiing. I hit a rock or something," Jill stammered.

"You alone?" he demanded to know.

"No," Jill never lied, but fear compelled her to be less than truthful. "My husband is with me. He'll be back soon. He went to get help."

"You were calling out for Tom. Is that your husband's name?"

"Yes. Now put me down."

Ignoring her command, he continued, "Doesn't look like he's going to make it anytime soon. Jake and I have been out here for almost four hours and we haven't seen anybody. We'll have to wait until this storm lets up before we can travel anyway, so we'll see if that man of yours shows up."

Fear raised its ugly head once more. The man was not alone. Where was this Jake he was talking about? How was she possibly going to get away from them? Her head was pounding and the pain in her leg was excruciating.

The man laid her back down on the ground, very gently much to Jill's surprise. He walked to the mule tied to a nearby tree.

"Easy now, boy," he spoke softly to the nervous animal trying to pull the reins loose from a branch. "This should let up soon. We'll be home before you know it." He ran a hand down the animal's neck, reached into one of the packs hanging from the side of the mule and withdrew a bright red stocking cap, a brown wool blanket and an old army canteen.

Jill watched the large man coming toward her. Once next to her, he lowered himself to his haunches. Placing one hand behind her neck, he held the canteen to her lips.

"Take it slow," he cautioned.

The cool liquid tasted good as it trickled over her lips and down her into her throat. She began to shiver as the cold wind permeated her jeans and a winter jacket meant more for looks than warmth. Since she didn't plan to stay more than a couple of days at the cabin, she hadn't brought many clothes.

The man brushed the snow from Jill's hair and pulled the stocking cap over her head. He reached for the blanket, wrapped part of it over her and anchored it under her side. Then he lay down next to her. When he began to pull her body close, she protested but he ignored her and tucked the remaining part of the blanket around himself.

"This should keep us warm until the storm lets up and we can get to my cabin."

His cabin? Why would he take her to his cabin instead of the hospital? No one would be able to find her there. Fear squeezed until she couldn't breathe. She fought the blackness beginning to surround her. She needed to be awake, alert. It was hard to tell what this man might have in mind for her.

"I'm David Tanner. Most people just call me Tanner. What's your name?"

Tanner tried to get the woman to talk, hoping she would stay conscious, but she only mumbled, "Look more like Goliath," and passed out.

Even through the clothing separating them, Tanner could feel the shapely contours of a woman's body as he held her close. One cheek lay on his shoulder; the other was covered by long, black hair that delicately curled around her face as it poked out from beneath the stocking cap and cascaded to below her shoulders. He began to react to the sensations created by her closeness.

This just isn't going to work, he told himself as he rose and tucked the blanket back around her. *I've been alone too long in these mountains.*

He began to search for branches to use for splints. Finding

two that would work, he shook the snow from them, snapped them off the tree and sat down next to her. Using his whittling knife, he worked until they were smooth as a polished stone. He slit through her denim jeans and exposed the broken leg.

Quickly, Tanner unhooked the leather strings from his boots and used them to anchor the splints to her leg. This was no place to set a leg. It would have to be done after he reached the cabin.

Tanner gently picked Jill up and put her over his shoulder like he was carrying a sack of flour. He walked to the mule, untied the reins from the branch and carefully mounted, sliding her down into the cradle of his arms.

"Come on, Jake, let's head for home. Looks like her husband isn't going to make it back for a while and I don't intend to freeze to death waiting for him."

~~~~~~~~

Melissa stood staring at the cabin, unsure what to do. Jill's car was here, but she didn't answer the door. Was Jill still so angry she was never going to talk to her? She pounded on the door again. Still no one answered. Snow was falling heavily now and even though Jill needed to know the truth, Melissa wasn't going to wait around and get caught in the storm. She would catch up with Jill when she returned to Knoxville.
~~~~~~~~

CHAPTER 2

The snow formed into hard small pellets bombarding Tanner's face like BB's. They stung as they hit the soft skin around his eyes and lodged in the beard covering the majority of his face. He covered the woman with the heavy army blanket, leaving nothing of her face or body exposed.

Unable to see anything through the blinding snow, Tanner left the reins slack and concentrated on holding the limp body. His arms ached and his fingers were numb from the cold, but it shouldn't be long before they reached the cabin. He was counting on the mule's keen sense of home to get them there.

The mule stopped moving. He raised his head, listening. His ears twitched back and forth several times. Then his lips curled upward and with a strange grin-like appearance large teeth were exposed. The mule began to bray. An answering bray came from a short distance away.

"Jake, you old fool; you took us to Tuttle's. I guess this is still home to you. Take us on in then. We can at least get warmed up before we go on."

The surefooted animal made its way down a rocky incline into a clearing filled with cabins.

A greeting party of one, a young man carrying a pail full of milk, met them. "What ya doin' out in a storm like this, Davey? What ya got wrapped in thet blanket?"

"A woman and she's been hurt. Will you get your pa to help me get her inside, Toby?"

"Sure will." Toby ran to the nearest cabin, gingerly holding the pail in such a way as to not spill any milk. Moments later he returned with a man almost as large as Tanner.

"Careful, Ned, her leg is broken," Tanner cautioned as he placed the woman into the other man's arms. Then he eased himself off the mule.

Ned took a quick peak under the blanket at the woman hidden beneath it. He issued orders as he strode toward the cabin. "Toby, see to the mule. Davey, come inside and have a little shine to warm up yer insides."

The fragrance of meat, vegetables and freshly baked bread wafted toward Tanner as Maybelle opened the door and asked, "Who ya got there, Davey?"

"I don't know who she is, but she took a nasty fall and broke her leg."

"Carry her back to Toby and Zeke's room, Ned," Maybelle ordered her husband.

Tanner pulled back the curtain covering the doorway and held it while Ned entered and laid the woman on a small cot.

"She oughta fit fine on this small bed. She doesn't look bigger than a mite herself. Where did ya find her, Davey?" Ned questioned as Maybelle began to remove the young woman's coat.

"Up on Bear Ridge. Said she was skiing and fell." Tanner pulled off his gloves and began to rub his hands together to help stop the stinging. "I've got to get warmed up before I set her leg."

"There's stew in the pot and fresh bread on the cupboard. Have yerself some supper before ya come back in, Davey," Maybelle offered. "I'll git her outa these wet clothes."

"Here, have a swig of this." Ned set a brown jug on the table, grabbed a towel hanging from a large nail protruding from the wall above the linoleum covered countertop and handed it to Tanner. "Ya kin use this to wipe off the drippin's."

Tanner wiped his face and ran the cloth down the length of his hair several times trying to remove the balls of ice stuck in it. Shoving the brown jug back to Ned, he said, "Thanks, but I need to keep a clear head." It wasn't just that he couldn't drink now, since he committed his life to the Lord he no longer wanted, or needed, to drink anything alcoholic.

Maybelle's voice could be heard coming from the other room; she was talking but getting no response. How long it would take for the young woman to regain consciousness was anybody's guess. Tanner wondered how she was going to respond when she found out her husband had not returned for her. Leaving his injured wife alone wasn't a smart move. He could easily have gotten lost in the blinding snow. Even a veteran mountaineer would have trouble finding his way in this storm.

He heard the woman cry out for Tom.

"Who's Tom?"

Hearing Ned's question, Tanner looked up. He was so wrapped up in his own thoughts he had forgotten about the man sitting next to him at the table. Neither had he noticed Toby's return.

"Before she lost consciousness, she mentioned a husband who went for help. It must be him."

"How's he gonna find her now you brung her here?" asked Toby.

Ned reached over and ruffled the young man's red hair. "Ain't none of yer business, son. Now gather up the rest of the youngin's so we can eat the vittles yer ma fixed."

Tanner mopped up the remains of the rabbit stew on his plate with a huge chunk of bread thickly spread with homemade butter. He leaned back in his chair and gave a sigh of contentment. His rest was short. It was time to set a broken leg.

"Has she come to yet?" he asked as he entered the cramped quarters of the small room.

"Sorta. Comes around for a few minutes, and then passes out agin," Maybelle responded. "Just keeps callin' fer somebody named Tom. Musta cracked her head pretty hard. There's a lump the size of a crab apple above her left ear. Wouldn't have seen it 'cept I was washin' her face and saw some blood next to her hairline. All that hair kinda covered it up."

Tanner's large fingers slid through thick, curly, black hair searching for the lump. His eyes scanned the delicate features of a porcelain doll face splattered with freckles across nose and cheekbones.

He moved the blanket and discovered Maybelle had dressed the woman in a pale blue cotton nightgown. Bright red leggings had been slipped over both legs. One bulged from the splint beneath it.

"Maybelle, have you got any plaster of Paris left?"

"You mean the stuff you gave the kids to make molded animals?"

"Yes, that's it."

"Yep, they didn't use it all."

"Good. Would you bring me a pan of warm water along with

the plaster? Get some old bed sheets and tear them into strips. I could use some of that cheesecloth you use when you're making jelly, too, if you don't mind parting with a little of it."

Maybelle left the room to gather up the necessary equipment. Tanner removed the legging, then the splint. Purple coloring had begun to surround a reddened area halfway between her knee and ankle. It looked like a clean break.

"Oh-h-h-h." Jill's head felt as if someone was pounding on it with a sledgehammer. Fingers were probing around on her leg. She opened her eyes slowly. A strange man stood bent over her, his face concealed by long blonde hair that fell over it. He turned toward her. Now she remembered the mountain man. But where was she? And what was he doing to her?

His hands remained on her leg. Blue eyes pierced hers.

"How are you feeling?"

The gruffness of his voice belied the softness of the words. Jill searched his face for a sign to take away the fear welling up inside her. There was none.

What she did see was furrows creasing his forehead from the scowl surrounding his eyes. Eyes that seemed large and intimidating on a face almost totally covered with hair. Jill had never seen such a massive beard. Its curly, golden hair stood out at least an inch from his cheeks and bushed around where Jill thought his chin should be, descending down a thick neck and disappearing beneath his shirt collar.

From what Jill had been told about the men who lived high in the mountains, she should be afraid. And she was. Yet, at the same time, she felt safe. It made no sense at all.

Again he asked how she felt. She responded, "Like I fell off the top of a mountain." Before she could say anymore a woman entered the room. In one hand she carried a large box, in the other she gingerly balanced a wooden bowl filled with water.

Draped over one arm were various strips of brightly colored cotton material.

A huge smile lit up Maybelle's face as she observed Jill. "Well, I see ya finally came to. That's good. Ya been standin' on the edge of up yonder fer quite a spell." Maybelle placed everything she brought into the room on a small table and pushed it over to the side of the bed where Tanner stood.

Jill studied the woman. She was tall and big-boned. Her plain face had a wholesome, rosy glow to it, making her look almost pretty. Braids angled down each side of her head meeting at the nape of her neck to form a circle. A powdery, white substance clung to the blue cotton dress where her stomach protruded. It was obvious the woman was going to have this mountaineer's baby very soon.

"It's time." Tanner ordered Maybelle, "You grab her shoulders and hold her down."

"No! Wait! What are you going to do?" Jill struggled to get up from the bed.

The man pushed her back down. "We have to get your leg set. This is going to hurt so I suggest you grab a tight hold on the mattress. Maybelle, give her something to bite into so she won't scare the youngin's half to death by screaming."

"Oh…" was all Jill was able to get out before the woman stuffed a knotted rag into her mouth. Then she used her large hands to cover Jill's upper arms and pin them to the bed.

Tanner's hands gripped her leg and quickly snapped the bone back in place. Explosions of bright flashing lights filled Jill's eyes. Pain radiated from the tips of her toenails clear up to the top of her head.

"She's out agin, Davey." Maybelle smoothed dampened hair away from Jill's face. "Poor little thing. That musta pained her somethin' awful. What's her name?"

"I don't know."

"Well, then, where's her kin live?"

"I don't know that either. Now will you quit asking me questions and help me get this cast made? Wet the strips in the bowl, ring the water out of them and hand them to me."

He began just below Jill's knee, angling each wide strip of cloth to circle around and down the leg. He continued to add strips until he reached her ankle, where he stretched it under the bottom of the foot and over the top several times, securing the loose end by tucking it inside another part of the cloth. Next, dampened cheesecloth was wrapped around the leg in the same fashion.

"I'll mix up the plaster while you put something under her leg to protect the bedding," Tanner said. "This is going to be pretty messy."

Maybelle pulled an old ragged-looking quilt from beneath the bed and carefully slid it under the wrapped leg.

A soft, gray substance squished through Tanner's fingers as he added water to the plaster and mixed it with his hands. "Thanks, Maybelle. I can finish this alone now. Why don't you go have some supper and rest for a while? How are you feeling?" Wistfulness filled Tanner as he watched Maybelle pat her tummy. He thought about the children he had wanted. Some things just weren't to be.

"Jest fine 'cept for this babe kicking like a mule tied to a fence post with a polecat comin' at it."

Tanner laughed loudly. Sometimes he was still surprised by the way the mountaineers said things. "I'm glad you're feeling good. We'll be moving out come first light in the morning. The cast should be set by then."

"Yer more than welcome to stay right here, ya know."

"I know Maybelle, and thanks. But I think it would be best if we go to my place."

Tanner scooped up two hands-full of the gooey plaster and began smoothing it over the cloth wrappings. His large hands circled her small leg with enough room left over so that his thumbs could overlap his fingers by the full length of each one. He finished with the plaster at her ankle.

There were no signs of her coming to yet. Dark eyelashes spiked out onto her cheeks from eyes that remained closed. Her chest moved in the rhythmic breathing of one who is in a deep sleep.

The cotton nightgown Maybelle had dressed the young woman in had twisted and bunched around the top of her legs. Tanner wiped the plaster from his hands and reached for the gown's hem.

Jill suddenly woke feeling like something was wrong. She looked down. Her nightgown had been pulled up. The man's hands were still on it. She screamed.

CHAPTER 3

Tanner didn't see Jill's eyes open; he only heard the scream. *She thinks I'm going to attack her,* he realized as he quickly clamped his hand over her mouth. Eyes wide with fear stared at him.

"I wasn't trying to…" Tanner didn't know what to say. He suddenly felt guilty for the thoughts entering his mind earlier as he had looked her over from head to toe. "I was only going to pull your gown down. Do you understand? I'll move my hand away if you promise not to scream again."

Jill looked into eyes only inches away from hers. They seemed softer now, not so hard and cold. Could she have been wrong about his intentions? Maybe. She had to admit he had done nothing to harm her….so far, unless she counted the pain he inflicted while setting her leg.

She nodded her head. The large hand covering the bottom half of her face moved away. He went to the bottom of the bed, retrieved a brightly colored quilt and silently covered her with it.

"What's goin' on in here? Ya tryin' to kill her off already, Davey?"

Jill turned her head to see another man almost as large as the one standing by her bed. He had a square build with huge muscles bulging from arms tightly covered by a faded blue shirt. A beard also covered his face. Hazel colored eyes sparkled from beneath black eyebrows that matched long, thick, black hair. She recalled the name Jake having been mentioned. Could this be him?

The blonde giant spoke to the other man, but his eyes stayed connected to Jill's, as if he were asking her to go along with what he said. "Nothing, Ned. She's okay now. She just woke up frightened of the unfamiliar surroundings. I doubt if she appreciates your sense of humor."

"Well, wakin' up to the looks of a fella like you standin' over 'em would scare anybody to their Maker." Ned chuckled as he swept the curtain aside and left the room.

Tanner grabbed a wooden chair from the corner, pulled it beside the bed and sat down. The woman lying in the bed looked so tiny, so fragile. Yet, she hadn't complained of the pain she had to be feeling. He wished there was something he could give her to ease it. Maybe a little of Ned's moonshine would help, but first he needed to find out more about her.

"What's your name?"

"Jill." She watched as the man crossed one leg over the other, ankle resting on knee, his large hands curled over the leg as if holding it in place. Pants made of some kind of tanned animal skin stretched tightly over legs almost as big around as her waist. He leaned back in the chair, causing it to squeak as if it were complaining about the heavy load forced upon it.

"Jill what?" Tanner wondered if he was going to have to squeeze information out of her one word at a time.

"Jill Morgan. And who are you?"

"My name is David Tanner, but you can call me Tanner."

"Davey. Isn't that what that man, Ned, called you?"

Tanner smiled. She didn't look so afraid of him now. An impish smile reached her eyes. Eyes as dark and soft as warm hot fudge. *Watch out*, he warned himself, *this dark haired beauty could get under your skin real fast and the last thing you need is more woman trouble. Besides, she's married.* Which brought up the question of why she hadn't asked about her husband?

"The Tuttle clan nicknamed me after the famous Davey Crocket. They say wild animals just stop and wait for me to shoot them. Kinda like the old folk tale claiming when Crocket aimed his rifle at a raccoon in a tree, it recognized him and said, 'Don't shoot, Colonel. I'll come down. I know when I'm a gone coon.'"

Jill couldn't help laughing at Tanner's tale, but when she did it made her head hurt. She reached up to rub the tender spot causing the pain. She wasn't sure which was worse, her aching head or the pain in her leg. Actually, her whole body hurt.

She remembered the helpless feeling of being in mid-air, knowing she was going to crash to the ground, but unable to do anything about it. She also remembered the fear she felt when she first saw this big, hairy mountain man.

She let her guard down a second ago by laughing at his story. She wouldn't do it again, she had to be careful. He still hadn't told her what he planned on doing with her. Nothing had been said about getting her to a hospital or taking her home.

Tanner watched Jill's light laughter turn into a grimace of pain. "I'll get you something for the pain. It's not exactly prescription pain-killer, but it may help some."

As he left the room, Jill wondered about this man, Tanner. He didn't use the same hill jargon as the other man and woman.

He talked more like someone who was educated. If that were so, what was he doing living here on the mountain? Questions, she had so many of them. Maybe she would feel less afraid if she knew the answers. Or maybe she just wanted to know more about this intriguing man.

Thoughts went to the men she had met over the last year. None of them interested her. Why would this man? He had the look of a wild animal and the gruffness of a caveman. Trying to tame him would be more than a challenge.

Tame the man! What was she thinking? But before Jill could analyze her thoughts, Tanner returned to the room carrying a small brown jug. He pulled the cork from the top and handed the jug to Jill.

"Try a few sips of this. It may help ease the pain."

Jill propped herself up on her left elbow. Then, trying to remember how she had seen hillbillies on television grab hold of a jug of moonshine and sling it over their shoulder to drink, she hooked her right thumb and forefinger around the curved handle and tried to imitate them, but failed since the jug kept slipping off her shoulder. Finally, she just tipped the jug up to her mouth and took a drink. The liquid created such an intense heat in her throat she was afraid to swallow. When she did, it felt as if fire engulfed her insides. Tears streamed from her eyes. Words caught in her throat as she tried to get them out, "T-t-t-that's a-a-awful."

Tanner wanted to reach over and wipe the tears from her eyes; instead he pushed the jug back up to her mouth. "Drink a little more. Trust me, it will help."

"Trust you?" Jill couldn't believe what she was hearing. She was being asked to trust a man she knew nothing about. One who appeared to be trying to get her intoxicated with this vile liquor.

"Come on, drink some more. Or are you afraid of what you might do if you get a little loose?" He grinned as he watched Jill's expression change. The challenge worked.

"Of course not. I've never been loose, as you call it, in my life. I don't drink."

"I thought not. You seem like the straight-laced Victorian type to me."

In answer to what appeared to be an insult, Jill tipped the jug up to her lips once more. It still burned going down. Tears formed in her eyes again. But there was no way she was going to let him know it.

"I may be sensible. Cautious, even. But I am *not* Victorian." Even as the denial came from her lips, Jill realized what Tanner said was true. She was straight-laced. She never let her emotions show. She held them tightly inside.

She even dressed in a Victorian style. Her necklines never plunged, her skirt hems never rested above her knees. Once, just once, it might be fun to let go, to not worry about anything except enjoying the moment.

Jill tipped the jug again. It wasn't so bad this time. A few more sips and she would have proven to him she could handle it. She watched a wide grin spread across his face. Due to all the hair on his face, the only part of a grin could be seen, causing crinkling around his eyes. "What's so funny?" she asked.

"Nothing, but I think you've had enough. Or are you going to drink it all just to prove you can?"

"No. Sorry. Here you are." Words were having trouble being formed by Jill's lips. The heavy jug almost slipped from her fingers as she passed it to Tanner.

Jill leaned back onto the pillow. She didn't hurt anymore. In fact, she couldn't feel anything, except the heaviness of the cast on her leg. She felt light, like she was floating on a cloud.

Giggles erupted from her as she imagined herself lying on a cloud with her cast leg dangling down from it. People below were looking up and pointing, questioning what was hanging out of the clouds.

Tanner pulled the covers up to Jill's chin. "Try to get some sleep. We'll be leaving early in the morning."

"M-m-mm. Leaving." Jill snuggled further down under the heavy quilt. Though she didn't really care, she asked, "Where are we going?"

"My place."

"Your place. Sounds…" Her eyes drifted shut. Something didn't seem quite right, but it didn't matter. She was too tired to think about it now.

When her dream began, she was once again on a cloud. Only this time the big man, Tanner, and her son Alex were with her. Tanner was holding her close, saying, "Trust me. I won't let you fall. I won't ever let anything hurt you again." Then, without another word, he pushed Alex off the cloud. He was tumbling through the air. Swiftly, the ground was rushing toward him, but there was nothing Jill could do to save him as Tanner held on to her tightly. She shouted, "No, Alex, don't leave me."

Tanner was cleaning up the mess he had made with the plaster. *Who the heck was she calling out for now? She had told him her husband is Tom, so who is Alex?*

CHAPTER 4

Jill woke up to the sound of a door slamming, then pots and pans rattling over the voice of Maybelle humming a tune she didn't recognize.

Her view through the window at the foot of the bed was unhampered by a valance strung across its top. Stars shone brightly in the darkened sky. A quarter moon hung low enough to give the impression it was about to collide with the tops of the giant pine trees staggered on the hillside.

She lay quietly listening to the sounds of children's voices as they spoke to Maybelle in hushed tones. Dawn began to inch its way across the horizon. Bright hues of pink and purple replaced the stars.

Recalling an old saying about a red sky in the morning being a sailor's warning, she wondered if more bad weather was coming and what this day would bring.

A feeling of loneliness swept over her. She missed her son, but was glad he was in good hands. She was in a strange place with even stranger people and unable to get herself out of the situation. She had always been able to figure a way out of troublesome spots before. Now she was unable to come up with a solution. The broken leg would hamper moving anywhere under her own power for a while, plus she had no clue how to find her way off the mountain.

The door slammed once again, breaking her train of thought. Feet stamped. The high-pitched voice of a young man spoke, "Pa and Davey will be in shortly, Ma. They're riggin' up a sling-type thing on Jake fer the lady's leg. Seems to me, it'd be easier fer them ta just stay here fer a spell. 'Specially since the snow's higher than a coon dog's tail."

Maybelle answered the boy, "Yup, son, I agree, but you know Davey. Once he sets his mind ta somethin', there ain't no changin' it. In the three years I've known him….."

The rest of what Maybelle said was drowned out by the sound of others entering the cabin and stamping their feet. At least she now knew Maybelle wasn't Tanner's wife.

She could hear his deep voice describing what he and Ned had rigged up on the mule so her broken leg wouldn't have to hang down on the ride to his cabin.

Dimly she recalled Tanner telling her last night they were leaving this morning, but no way was she going to be alone with him at his place. She would find a way home, with or without his help. She had no intention of spending even one minute more alone with that man.

Her eyes focused on a hand moving the curtain and a head ducking in order to enter through a doorway that was too short. She watched lips curve into a slow, lazy smile as Tanner neared her bed. In his hand was a bowl filled with oatmeal. Milk floated around the edges of the bowl and a small pile of what Jill assumed was maple sugar sat in the middle.

Tanner mixed in the milk and sugar, then picked up a spoonful and directed it toward Jill's mouth. "You'd better eat this, then we'll get ready to move out."

Jill shoved his hand away, spilling the mixture on the quilt covering her. "I don't want any. And even if I did, I am perfectly capable of feeding myself. It's my leg that's broken, not my arm."

Tanner was amused and a little impressed by Jill's fiery display of independence. She certainly was different from any other women he knew. Most of them would relish being waited on, but not this one.

He took a piece of cloth from the table and wiped up the oatmeal she spilled. The sensation his hand created left her feeling a little breathless. His eyes suddenly turned cold as he shoved the bowl at her.

"Eat this. I'll get Maybelle to help you get dressed." Quickly Tanner left the room. The woman was too tempting. How he was going to be able to keep his distance when they were alone, he didn't know. He only knew he had to, for both their sakes.

Jill watched broad shoulders and narrow hips hastily exit the room. She wondered if he, too, was fighting the magnetic pull that seemed to be drawing them together. Opposites attract, and they were about as opposite as it could get.

"How ya doin'?" Maybelle's motherly inquiry was followed by a brush of her hand across Jill's forehead and the top of her head. The natural warmth of this woman made Jill feel comfortable with her. She watched the fabric of Maybelle's dress move as the baby she was carrying gave a few lively kicks.

"I'm fine. I remember when my son, Alex, used to kick me like that. It felt like I had a heavyweight boxer inside trying to fight his way out. When is your baby due?"

"In a couple of weeks. How old is yer youngin'?"

"Four." Then Jill added sadly, "I sure miss him. I shouldn't have come up here."

"Why did ya come?" Maybelle's curiosity needed to be satisfied. After all, Davey was taking Jill to his place. When cousin Julie Ann found out, the questions were bound to fly, and some fur, she imagined.

Julie Ann had set her sights on Davey when he first came up the mountain. The only thing stopping her from hogtying him into marriage was her pa. The old man refused to let Julie Ann marry up with him. He claimed Davey wasn't clan and no matter how long he lived on the mountain he would still be city folk and everybody knows they can't be trusted.

Maybelle didn't know about city folk, she had never been off the mountain. But she and her family not only trusted Davey, they loved him. Maybelle thought there wasn't a kinder man in the hills, except for her Ned, of course.

When Jill saw the questioning look on Maybelle's face she decided to explain but without going into detail about her father. "I came for some peace and quiet, and to sort through some problems in my life. My husband died suddenly a year ago. Not only did I have to deal with his death, but numerous financial problems as well.

"Unknown to me, he cashed in his life insurance policy for part of the money to start our business. We had only been operating a few months when he died. We weren't making a profit yet, so the mortgage payments on our home were more than I could afford.

"I ended up selling our home and moving in with a friend and her two children. This past year has been a continual fight to keep a roof over our heads and the business going. I guess it took its toll. My friend, Carrie, insisted I take some time off to rest." This was true, even though wasn't the only reason Jill came to the cabin.

"I see," Maybelle said. But the only part of Jill's story she understood was about her husband dying. Life insurance, mortgages, what was all that stuff? "Let's see if'n these clothes will work. I know the pants are too big, but ain't much gonna fit over that plastered leg of yers."

Tanner sat at the side of the table near the curtained door. Jill and Maybelle's conversation could be easily heard. Now he knew why she had not asked about her husband, he was dead. Now, he knew Alex was her son, but still, she lied to him. Why would a woman say her husband had gone for help when he had been dead for a year?

Could there have been another man with her? It really didn't matter to him. He would take care of her until it was possible to get her down off the mountain, then he would never see her again. With a child at home and a business to run, it wasn't too likely she would ever come back up the mountain.

He wasn't ever going back to live in the city again, that was for sure. He liked his life here on the mountain. It got a little lonely at times, but all he had to do was come over to the Tuttle's for a while and he was ready for the peace and quiet of his own place once more. He hunted, he fished, and he lived off the land. Just as his grandfather had done so many years ago.

The sound of Maybelle's voice roused him from his thoughts. "We're ready, Davey. Ya kin come in now."

Tanner choked down the laughter threatening to escape when he saw the small woman literally swimming in pants half a dozen sizes too large for her. Jill's tiny waist was cinched with a piece of twine strung through the belt hoops of the denim jeans, creating enough bulging material from waist to hips that several fluffy pillows could have easily fit into.

The bottom of each pant leg was neatly folded up several turns, giving them a wide-cuffed look. The pink cowl neck of Jill's own sweater hung outside the top of a red wool shirt snugly buttoned. The contrast of small to big looked hilariously funny. Tanner could hold his laughter no longer.

"Just what is so funny?" Jill knew she didn't exactly look like the belle of the ball, but there was no need for him to make her feel any more ridiculous than she already did.

"You look like a clown. Your face just needs some white grease paint, a big red nose and big red lips and you would be all set for the circus."

Tanner stared at Jill's lips. They weren't big; instead they were delicately heart shaped. They weren't red, but rather a soft pink. He wondered how they would feel touching his lips. His eyes met hers.

Was the look he was getting challenging him to kiss her? He didn't know. What he did know was he didn't dare find out. Getting involved with this woman would definitely change his life. And he didn't want or need any more changes.

Maybelle stood back watching the exchange of looks between Davey and Jill. It was easy to see the sparks flying between them. It would be interesting to see if this little mite of a woman could capture the heart of the reclusive man.

Maybelle figured Davey had been hurt badly by someone because he acted so standoffish to women. She also knew that once a man's pride was stomped on he drew up inside himself and refused to open his heart again. It would take a very special woman to break through David Tanner's reserve.

CHAPTER 5

"It's time to go. Put this on." Tanner held out Jill's coat to her.

"I'm not going. I'm staying right here." The pillows stacked behind her helped Jill sit upright in the bed. Her arms stayed crossed tightly across her chest, verifying her refusal.

She looked at Maybelle, hoping she would back her up and say it was alright for Jill to stay. But she said nothing, only gave Jill a weak smile. Apparently these mountain women went along with however the men said it was going to be. Well, she wasn't going along with it. She wasn't going anywhere.

"No, you're not. You're coming with me." Tanner wished this woman would shut up and come along without arguing. Ned and Maybelle had enough mouths to feed without hers. With Maybelle so close to having her baby, the last thing she needed was to play nursemaid to some spoiled little city gal who didn't know the first thing about how these people lived.

It was a hard life. There were no automatic washers and dryers to do the laundry. It was all boiled in a pot and scrubbed on a board using soap they made themselves. There were no grocery stores around the corner where you could pick up a few things for a quick meal. All their food was either raised in their gardens, gathered from the woods, hunted or trapped.

There were no clothing stores from which they could buy ready-made clothes. With the exception of an occasional bolt of calico or denim fabric, their clothes were hand-made from the wool of their sheep or of tanned animal hides.

There was no indoor plumbing, no running water, and no electricity. But he couldn't say all this to Jill with Maybelle standing right beside him. They were a proud people, these mountaineers, and it wouldn't do to make them think you were insulting their way of life.

Tanner reached down, slid Jill's arms into the coat's sleeves, pulled it up around her shoulders and zipped it. His eyes bored a hole in hers, commanding her not to say another word. He slipped his right arm beneath her knees; his left arm went across her shoulder blades, his left hand wrapped around her rib cage beneath her arm.

Jill could feel Tanner's fingers tighten their grip around her as he lifted her from the bed. Her side was pressed against his buckskin jacket. Even through the thick clothing that separated them, she could feel a heart pounding. Was it his or hers? She wasn't sure.

She turned her face toward his, about to resist once more. The hard look on his face stopped her. There was nothing more she could do or say, he was forcing her to go with him. Whether she wanted to or not, apparently didn't matter to him.

Tanner could sense her glaring eyes focusing on his, but this time he didn't look into them. He didn't acknowledge the trembling lips only a hair's breadth away from his. Instead he looked straight ahead and started walking to the door. There would be time to explain later. “Maybelle, would you get the curtain?”

Maybelle held the curtain aside as Tanner ducked through the doorway, then moved in front of him, stopping his stride toward the cabin’s outside door.

“Toby, git me a pair of mittens and a hat,” she called to the boy using a poker in the fireplace to stir up the fire.

“Yes, ma,” the boy replied as he hurried to a wooden box near the door and retrieved mittens and a hat.

Six pair of curious children’s eyes regarded Jill from their places at the table as Maybelle put thick, hand-crocheted gray mittens on her hands and a matching hat on her head.

Jill felt like a child herself. She gulped back tears threatening to burst from her and took several long, deep breaths to try and regain control of her emotions. Tanner’s giant arms wrapped around her, tightened, then loosened, as if they had given her a small hug. “It will be alright,” was whispered next to her ear.

She turned her face toward him and gazed into eyes with a softened, concerned look in them. Confused by the unfamiliarity of raw emotion and the power this man seemed to have over her, she wondered how she could hate him one moment and feel so attracted to him the next.

Jill looked away from the magnetic eyes drawing her into them. She focused her attention once more on the quiet group at the table. She couldn’t remember ever having seen so many children be so quiet. When her son, Alex, and Carrie’s two boys were together the racket coming from them was almost deafening.

Tanner swung Jill around to face a row of pegs on the wall. “Grab my cap, will ya?”

Jill reached for the coonskin cap, set it on Tanner’s head and gave it a twist so the tail would hang down the center of his back.

Ned got up from his spot at the table. He grabbed a buckskin coat from one of the pegs and walked to the door. “I’ll he’p ya git her into thet rig.”

As they walked out the door, Jill called over Tanner’s shoulder, “Thank you, Maybelle. I hope I get a chance to see you again.”

She watched as numerous heads appeared at the window. The children steamed the glass with their breath, drawing pictures in the cloudy moisture. She remembered doing the same thing as a child and being told by her mother to stop smearing up the windows.

Maybelle joined the children in their artwork and drew the shape of a house. One child put in windows, another the door, and a third drew smoke curling from a chimney. Jill felt envious. These people seemed to have such a peaceful life, so far removed from the stress-filled one she lived.

Tanner stopped walking. Jill turned her head away from the window and saw a mule with the strangest looking contraption she had ever seen anchored to it. It had a backrest and small wooden poles running down each side. Another pole went across the mule’s head behind its ears and then was joined to the side poles. Burlap was attached to the poles and hung hammock style across the animal’s back and up the backrest.

Tanner set her on the saddle. Ned gently lifted her legs into the hammock, then pulled a piece of rope from the pocket of his coat and handed it to Tanner, who wrapped it around her middle and tied it behind the backrest.

“You don’t have to tie me up. I’m not going to run away,” Jill said sarcastically as she shifted around trying to get comfortable.

“I’m not tying you up. I’m tying you on, so you won’t fall off.” Tanner reached over to the fence and retrieved a blanket.

He laid it over Jill's legs and tucked it in around them. "This should help to keep you warm."

Untying the reins from the fence, he gave them a light yank. "Come on, Jake. Let's go home. See ya later, Ned."

Tanner trudged through the deep snow, grateful for Jill's silence. It gave him a chance to think. The less she knew about him, the better. Women were naturally nosey. They would ask questions until they were satisfied they knew everything that ever happened to you from the day you were born. Very few people knew where he was and he planned to keep it that way.

The mountain people asked very few questions. They figure your life is your business and no one else's. That's exactly how Tanner intended to keep it. If she asked any questions, he would just tell her it was none of her business.

Jill looked up at the sky. It had turned from calm and bright to ominous. A gray look had descended on everything, even the white snow. She wondered how long it would take to get to Tanner's cabin, but was hesitant to ask. His back was to her. He hadn't said one word to her since they left Tuttle's. His pace was steady, breaking only when it was necessary to lead the mule around some obstacle in their path.

The hammock for her legs was meant to make it easier for her to travel, but with each step the mule took, Jill felt a searing pain in her leg. Her tailbone was sore from rubbing against the saddle and her face felt frozen into a permanent scowl.

Try to think of nice things, she told herself. But nothing would come to mind. Only questions. Questions about the man who was taking her to his cabin. Who was he? Where did he come from? Had he run away from some kind of trouble?

Was he a killer hiding out in the mountains? Was he going to kill her? No, Jill reasoned, he could have done it as soon as he found her instead of saving her.

What did he want with her then? Her mind was a jumble of thoughts skipping from one idea to another, landing on the memory of the way he looked at her, how he touched her. And the scene with her nightgown. Maybe he had really been pulling it up, not down as he told her.

"Oh, no," she murmured as realization and fear hit her. There had to be a way to get away from him. There had to be, but how?

"Did you say something?"

The sudden sound of his voice startled Jill. The mule stopped moving. Tanner was walking back toward her.

"With all this snow, it's pretty slow going. It will be quite a while before we get to my cabin." He reached into the side pack hanging off the mule's rump and pulled out a piece of cloth. "I'm hungry enough to eat the bark off a tree. Maybelle fixed us some sandwiches. Want one?" He unwrapped the sandwiches and handed her two pieces of bread spread with butter and filled with dark brown meat. It wasn't easy to handle with mittens on, but rather than let her hands get cold she managed to navigate it to her mouth. It was good, but the taste was different from anything with which she was familiar.

She studied the man standing beside the mule. She was going to have to ask some questions if she was ever going to find out what his intentions were. Maybe if she started off with little insignificant things he would start to open up.

"This is good. What is it?"

"Coon."

Jill choked on the bite she was chewing. "Coon? As in raccoon?" A picture of the cute mischievous looking animal with fox-like face, sharp pointed nose and black patches ringed in white around each eye kept her from eating any more of the sandwich.

"Yup." Laughter erupted from Tanner. "You probably just ate a cousin of the one whose tail is hangin' off the back end of my cap."

Jill threw the sandwich at him. "You think it's so funny, you eat it." It bounced off his bearded chin, leaving butter and small particles of meat stuck in the hair, then fell to the ground near his feet.

Tanner bent down, picked up the pieces of bread and meat scattered on the snow and put the sandwich back together. As he straightened up he used the back of his hand to wipe his face. The laughter was gone, seriousness replaced it. He held the sandwich out to her once again.

"You sure you don't want this?"

"I'm sure." She had made him angry, but she wasn't going to back down. She wasn't going to show him that she was afraid of him.

Tanner walked to the mule's head and grabbed the reins. "All I've got to say is you're going to get mighty hungry before we reach my place. This is all the food we have."

Jill watched as he opened his mouth and took a large bite of the sandwich. Then he turned his back to her and began walking.

CHAPTER 6

Jill heard a wild, terrifying cry, like the screaming of a woman in pain. The sound was coming from the tree just ahead. She looked up. A tawny-colored mountain lion crouched in the branches of the tree. With bared teeth and ears laid back, it leaped toward Tanner. Jill screamed, "Watch out, Tanner," just as he turned to face the cat's attack.

The mule kicked, then ran, bouncing Jill up and down on the saddle. She grabbed onto the saddle horn with one hand, with the other she covered her face to protect it from the tree branches swiping at her. The mule chose not to take the trail. Instead, it cut through the forest. The jarring of the mule's gallop sent shooting pains through her leg. After what seemed like an endless ride, the mule stopped and began chewing on branches of a leafless mulberry tree as if nothing had happened.

Darkness swirled before Jill's eyes. Tears of pain dripped to her cheeks. She had always been able to tolerate pain well, but right now all she wanted to do was scream. Instead, she grabbed the only part of her leg she could reach, her thigh, and quietly moaned.

The dizziness subsided, but the pain remained. The constant jarring of her leg must have caused more damage. It would probably have to be re-set.

Jill looked around. She was lost, alone and tied to the back of a mule. She didn't know if it would be better to stay on the mule and hope it would find its way home or to try and untie herself and get off. Before she could decide, the mule began to amble through the trees.

She tried to concentrate on something other than the pain in her leg. What about Tanner? Was he lying back there injured or dead? Even if the mule did find its way home, what then?

The sound of something moving in the trees behind her sent Jill's pulse racing. The backrest was in her line of vision and being tied the way she was made it impossible for her to lean around it.

Could the mountain lion be after her now? She had always heard big mountain cats didn't attack humans and they usually hunted for game at night. What was it doing out in the daylight and why did it attack Tanner? Then she remembered the circle of red blood flowing from high on the cat's right front leg. It had been shot. That might have something to do with why it attacked. If what she now heard was the mountain lion, she was in real trouble. She had no way of protecting herself.

"Jill."

The voice was distant, but Jill recognized it as Tanner's. Relief flooded her.

"Tanner? Where are you? Are you alright?"

"Tell that darned mule to stop so I can catch up to you."

"Whoa, Jake, whoa," Jill called out.

Tanner slowly came from behind. Stopping beside the mule, he forced a smile and lightly commented, "That's one for the record. I've never been attacked by a cat before."

Blood was streaming from a gash running from the outside corner of his left eye to the middle of his beard. His buckskin coat was ripped where dark red bloodstains marked the shoulders and sleeves. Deep claw marks marred the backs of his large hands.

"How did you get away? From the way the cat attacked, it looked like you didn't stand a chance of fighting it off with your bare hands."

"I didn't. I used my knife. It's too bad I had to kill it though. All the experts say there aren't any mountain lions left up here, there are a few in Louisiana and Florida, but most of them live out West now. Apparently they were wrong. Some hunter must have spotted this one and decided he wanted it for a trophy. He wasn't a very good shot and probably got too scared to try again if the cat came at him. Anyway the cat's injured leg worked to my advantage."

"From the way you look, I'd say it got in more than a few good licks."

"We had a pretty good tussle. It must have weighed at least 200 pounds. Even with an injured leg, it was strong. We better get going. We're way off the track and I have to go back and do something with the mountain lion."

"Why?"

"It's pretty obvious you're a city girl or you wouldn't ask a question like that. We don't waste anything here. The fur can be used for clothing and we can eat the meat."

Tanner grabbed the reins of the mule and turned the animal around. He smiled to himself, wondering if she would believe she was soon going to be eating mountain lion meat.

Jill's leg was hurting badly. All she wanted was to get somewhere, anywhere, so she could get off the mule and lie down. Her stomach churned at the thought of having to eat yet another wild animal. Raccoon was bad enough, but mountain lion…how disgusting!

They passed an opening between several large shrubs which looked like it might be a short cut back to where they came from. "Can't we go that way?"

Tanner looked to see where Jill was pointing. "Not unless you want to risk being lost for days. That's rhododendron. In some places it grows so thickly it's completely impenetrable. There's a story about a man named Huggins who was lost in a rhododendron thicket for days. When he finally staggered out to safety and was asked where he'd been, he said he didn't know for sure, but evidently he thought he had been in hell. That's why the mountaineers call those thickets "hells". Believe me; you don't want to get lost in one."

Tanner kept moving until he came to a narrow opening between the dense trees. As they threaded their way through, he wondered how the mule managed to get through there without knocking Jill, contraption and all, off his back.

A small brown rabbit dashed out of the trees and under the mule's feet, making it falter. The sudden motion caused intense pain in Jill's already aching leg.

"Oh-h-h."

Tanner looked back to see tears trickling from Jill's eyes and running down her bright red cheeks. He could see she was in pain and cold. Maybe he should have left her at Ned's. If it hadn't been for the mountain lion attacking and the mule running in the wrong direction, this trip would have been made in much less time.

He had to give the woman credit. She had a lot of grit. Not once had she complained. It was getting colder. His boots made a crunching noise with each step he took. The snow promised earlier by a murky sky began to fall. Large wet flakes clung to his mustache. He ran his tongue along the edge of his upper lip and captured the moisture of the snow. He was thirsty, cold and tired.

When they made it back to the trail, Jill could see the dead mountain lion sprawled across a fallen log a short distance ahead of them. A piercing whistle cut through the air sending a shivering, uneasy feeling up Jill's spine.

A large hawk, whose long, broad wings spanned at least 20 inches, flew down and, with a vise-like grip, sunk its sharp, curved talons into the cat's round head. Its light-colored beady eyes glared at them with fierce belligerence.

"Looks like she's trying to stake her claim." Tanner swung his arms and yelled at the bird, chasing it away. "I'll bury it here for now and come back for it later," he said as he dragged the cat off into the trees and covered it with snow.

"What made you call the hawk a she? Aren't the male birds the ones with that much color?" Jill asked as she watched the hawk return and land in the forked branch of a nearby tree.

"Some hawks have the same coloring whether male or female. Their world is quite different from ours. In theirs, the female is larger, stronger, and much bolder than the male. They waste nothing. They eat not only the flesh of birds and animals, but the bones and feathers or fur as well."

Tanner watched Jill's face crinkle up in the funny way she had of showing distaste. "There's a small cave just beyond this next bend. I'm going up there and see if it's empty so we can have some shelter and rest for a while. In case I should happen to wake a bear or two, I'm going to take you off Jake and leave you here. Old Jake doesn't like bears anymore than he did that cat. He'd more than likely take you for another wild ride. If he does run off, I'll find him later."

"You're going to leave me here alone? What if the bear, or

bears, decide to come this way? I can't exactly get up and run, you know." For a while Jill had thought this man might have some decency. Now he acted as if he didn't care whether bears ate her for lunch or not. Apparently he wanted to make sure the mule got away, even if she didn't.

Tanner moved to the back of the mule and untied the rope holding Jill to the backrest. He gently lifted her out of the saddle and placed her on top of a large drift of snow.

"Don't worry. I'll probably kill him before he gets to you. But just in case…." He walked to the side of the mule and removed a rifle from the sheath tied to the saddle. Three shells were removed from his buckskin pants pocket and slipped into the gun. He handed it to Jill.

"I don't know how to shoot that thing," Jill protested, but she slipped off her mittens, reached out and accepted the gun. Her left hand wrapped round the smooth, cold wood of the slender stock. Her right hand found the trigger guard; her forefinger touched the cold steel of the trigger. She wondered how much of a "hair-trigger" the rifle had and if her shaking finger could cause it to fire.

"Just aim for the biggest area, his chest. You shouldn't miss if you let him get close enough before you shoot."

With the gun laid across her blanket-covered lap, Jill watched Tanner saunter down the trail. She sat totally still, conscious of each sound in the forest. The resonant, drumming, rat-a-tat of a woodpecker's bill meeting the trunk of a 100-foot-tall, black walnut tree standing in front of her. A few crispy, dried leaves still attached to branches of a maple rustling in the wind. And the mule snorting as it breathed cold air through its large nostrils.

She watched snowflakes as they gracefully danced their way down to join those already wind-whipped into mounds on the ground. A reddish-brown fox stalked a cottontail rabbit, pouncing on it with lightening speed and running off into the forest with the rabbit dangling from its mouth.

She listened…she watched…. she waited.

CHAPTER 7

Tanner entered the dark, gloomy cave slowly. There was no sign of bears, but it never hurt to be cautious. Numerous small bats hung upside down by their feet from the rock ceiling, their wings draped around their bodies like Dracula's cloak. Most people said bats had the face of a mouse, but to him they looked like tiny bear's heads with long, pointed teeth. Their keen sense of hearing made them aware of Tanner's invasion and soon twittering squeaks of warning echoed through the cave as the bats flew out into the daylight.

With the little bit of light filtering in from the cave's opening and his eyes adjusting to the darkness, Tanner was soon able to scan the interior. It wasn't a large cave. Ice filled the cracks where water seeped in through the stone wall. An icicle-shaped stalactite hung from the ceiling and a stalagmite pillar rose from the floor, meeting to create a small column of stone on one wall.

Tanner walked back out, found a hollow log nearby, and with booted foot, kicked it until it broke into pieces. Little gray mice squeaked and scattered into the snow as their home was destroyed.

He returned to the cave, stood the dried wood tee-pee style near the back wall, and gathered up leaves that had blown in to put in the center of the tee-pee. He reached into the pocket of his coat and drew out a small tin box containing stick matches and said to no one, "I'm sure glad I don't live in the days when you had to do this by rubbing two sticks together."

After getting the fire started to warm the cave, Tanner headed back after Jill. He thought about her reaction to his telling her there might be bears in the cave. He chuckled to himself as he remembered the look she got on her face when he told her a hawk ate the flesh and bone of its prey, and her not being able to eat the raccoon meat. He knew it wasn't nice to tease her, but it sure was fun watching her face crinkle up in disgust and her dark eyes widen with fear. She wouldn't admit to fear, but her facial expressions told all.

Maybe he should make some growling sounds before he rounded the bend. No, not a good idea. She'd probably shoot him in the belly, then they would both die out here in the wilderness, and all because he was having a little fun with her.

"Jill, it's just me coming, no bears," he yelled as he rounded the bend. He watched her stiff upper body sag with relief and the tight grip she held on the gun pointed toward him relax.

Jill had heard the strange noises; a loud thumping, the sound of wood cracking; and the snow crunch, crunch, crunching with the movement of some creature on it, but she had heard no sound identifiable as human, until now. Her heart had been pounding, but now slowed to a normal beat. Her body, which felt like a balloon blown up to the point of exploding, now relaxed as the air she had been holding in her lungs escaped all at once.

"What took you so long?" Now that the crisis was past, Jill

was angry. It seemed as if this man enjoyed taunting her. Every time he mentioned what some wild creature might do, there was a gleam in his eyes and his lips slightly curled upward as if he were fighting to keep a huge grin from popping out.

"I started a fire to warm the cave up for you," he answered.

Now she felt guilty for mistrusting him. One minute she thought he was a cold and callous man, the next, kind and thoughtful. She wondered which was the real Tanner, or could he be a little of both?

Tanner took the gun from her hands, unloaded it and put it back in the sheath. The mule was still standing in the same place. He walked back to Jill, scooped her up in his arms and headed for the cave.

"Come on, Jake. Follow me," he said to the mule.

Jill watched in amazement as the animal plodded along behind them. It seemed to understand exactly what he said to it.

Her arms were around Tanner's neck, her fingers meeting on the warm, satiny skin near his Adam's apple. The hair of his long beard tickled the back of her hands. She was being carried off to a cave by a caveman-like giant. She knew she should be frightened, but she wasn't. A small shiver went through her body at the unwelcome thoughts she was having.

"Are you cold?"

"Uh-h. No." It was a good thing her cheeks were already rosy from the cold, maybe he wouldn't notice the blush that was creeping over them.

"You were shivering. The fire should help to keep you warm."

It felt good to have someone take care of her for a change. It seemed like all her life she had been the one to keep things going. Tom had been strong in the business world, but when it came to anything else in their life together, he had been insistent she make any necessary decisions. Maybe women caused fear in men by telling them repeatedly they want to be asked; they want their feelings and needs to be considered. These things were necessary, but when you got right down to it Jill thought most women wanted and needed a take-charge kind of man. *It must be a natural instinct that comes with us, for no matter how much we spout off about wanting to be independent, what we really want is to be able to be a little dependent some of the time, to feel secure "our man" will take care of us.*

Tanner lowered Jill to the ground next to the fire. The cave felt warm and cozy, like a romantic little hide-a-way secluded from the rest of the world. She watched as Tanner tucked the blanket around her legs. Once again she pushed away the silly romantic ideas invading her mind.

"I'm going to go see if I can round us up something to eat. You must be hungry since you didn't finish your sandwich and I'm starved enough to eat a bear—growl and all."

His reference to a bear reminded Jill this was a land filled with dangerous animals, almost as dangerous as the man standing in front of her who awakened something in her. Something she had been repressing for a long time. She remembered the first few months after Tom died and how she cried every night. She missed the soothing feeling of being held in someone's arms while falling asleep.

Jill realized Tanner hadn't moved, but was standing looking at her as if perplexed and a little worried. "You go on and do what you have to do," she told him. "I'll be fine."

Without a word, Tanner turned and left the cave, ducking as he moved through the low entrance. He found a fallen log and perched on it, quietly waiting and watching for some unsuspecting animal to come by and become their lunch, but his thoughts never left the woman in the cave. She appeared to be a strong woman, he liked that, but at the same time he sensed a vulnerability about her. He wondered if her life with her husband had been good. Did she miss him?

He still missed Emily, even though their marriage had gone through some rough times. His becoming a Christian, and trying to live the life of one totally mystified her. She fought him tooth and nail on giving away part of their income and volunteering to help those less fortunate. Thankfully, there had been enough time after they found out about her cancer for her to come to know the Lord before she died.

A fat brownish-gray rabbit hopped near him and stopped as if sensing danger. Its dark nose wiggled, trying to identify the scent. Its long, stand-up ears twitched and its big dark eyes looked at him pleadingly.

Jill heard the gun shot ring out. *You will eat whatever he brings with no qualms*, she told herself. *After all, you're in the wilderness and there is no other way to get food. This is how people used to live.* She thought of the Tuttle's and the others, including Tanner, who still lived off the land in these mountains. Well, if they could do it, so could she. At least for her it was a temporary thing, for them it was their way of life.

Tanner came back into the cave with the beheaded, skinned body of some small animal draped over one hand and a branch stripped of its bark in the other. He laid the meat down on a rock and stacked other rocks around the hot coals of the burned-downed pieces of wood. He pushed the stick through the center opening in the animal and laid each end of the stick on the stacked up rocks.

As the meat began to cook, it sent small drops of animal fat into the fire causing it to hiss and spit sparks. The surface of the meat became brown and the smell rising from it was mouth watering.

"I didn't know I was so hungry until I smelled the meat cooking." Jill tried to make conversation with the silent man who sat next to her and stared into the fire.

Tanner turned his head toward hers. His forehead was creased in a frown, his eyes interrogating. "Who was the man who went for help for you? I know it wasn't your husband because I overheard you telling Maybelle your husband died a year ago."

Jill was surprised by the question. She had totally forgotten about telling him her husband had gone for help. "There was no man."

"Then why did you tell me there was?"

"Because I was…well….afraid of you." She wasn't sure it was wise to admit being scared of him, but the eyes holding hers seemed to make lying impossible.

"Why were you afraid of me? I hadn't hurt you or threatened you in any way."

"You sounded so gruff and you looked mean. Besides, my friend, Carrie, told me to stay away from you mountain people. She said you didn't like strangers invading what you considered to be your domain and you were rough and ornery." Jill looked at the meat cooking over the fire and back to him, adding with a smile, "She also said you could shoot the eyes out of a squirrel at forty paces and rip the heart out of a bear with your bare hands and eat it raw."

His eyes hadn't left hers, but now a small boyish grin replaced the scowl on his face. "I'm surprised you came up here then, with all of us dangerous beasts running around."

"She told me it was safe as long as I stayed at the cabin and didn't wander off. I guess if I had listened to her I wouldn't have this broken leg."

"Nor would you be stuck in a cave alone with me."

CHAPTER 8

The minute the words were out of Tanner's mouth he regretted them. He did not want to be attracted to this woman and yet he was. They sat lost in the depths of each other's eyes until he drew her close for the kiss they both knew was about to take place. She reached her hand up to his shoulder, intending to draw him closer.

"Ouch!" Tanner removed Jill's hand from his shoulder. With an apologetic smile, he explained, "The cat must have torn me up a little more than I realized." He was relieved the kiss hadn't taken place. He was going to have to be much more careful around this beautiful woman in the future.

Jill turned away, embarrassed for letting herself reach out to this man. What was the matter with her? How could she have been ready to kiss a man she knew nothing about? A man living as if he were in the eighteenth century, imitating the dress and lifestyle of a pioneering Daniel Boone. He lived in the past; she was headed for the future. Falling in love with him would only bring her heartache. But then, she wasn't falling in love, it was purely an attraction to a ruggedly handsome man.

It reminded her of the stories she wrote as a teenager. She had gazed longingly at the mountains and created romantic stories about the people who lived there. But she wasn't a child anymore and she realized, in reality, it wasn't a glorious way to live. Instead it was a harsh one.

The entertainment she took for granted like movies, plays and concerts were something of which these mountaineers had no knowledge. Her whole way of life was based on doing things the quickest and easiest way with the best mechanical help available. Theirs was the hard way with everything being done by hand, from making their own clothes to raising their own food and hunting for meat.

Tanner took the meat from the fire and laid it on a rock to cool. He would have kissed her if the pain not stopped him. He knew it was wrong, but that didn't stop him from wanting. It was like having a fresh-out-of-the-oven apple pie sitting in front of you; its sweet, tangy scent wafting up, teasing and tormenting you with every breath to take just one little nibble.

Lord, help me to leave her alone, Tanner prayed. *She'll only bring trouble*. Immediately sorry for the thought, Tanner wondered how long it would take for his newly found Christianity to take affect so he could be kind and understanding. *Just keep working at it*, he told himself, *it's bound to happen someday.*

The meat was cool now. Tanner tore off a chunk and offered it to Jill. His hand touched hers as he laid the meat in her open palm. Neither looked into the eyes of the other, each afraid of the intense attraction they felt. They ate silently until Tanner stood and kicked dirt over the remains of the fire. "We better get going."

He's angry, Jill thought, as Tanner roughly picked her up and carried her to the mule. *He's pouting like a little boy. Well, let him pout*. She kept silent as he retied the rope around her and, with brisk steps, led the mule down the narrow trail.

The snow had stopped falling. The sun was darting in and out behind clouds covering all but tiny patches of blue sky here and there. Ice-coated trees glistened and birds sang, lending peacefulness to the solitude.

The narrow, tree-lined trail ended, opening up on a bluff with a panoramic view of snow-covered mountain peaks undulating across the horizon. Trees below looked like fat blades of green grass growing so tightly together a hair wouldn't fit between them.

Jill looked at the breathtaking view of mountain, cloud and blue sky meeting and forgot the long silence stretching out between them. "It's beautiful. I've lived barely an hour's drive from here all my life but have never been this high on the mountains."

"Right over there is where we're headed." Tanner pointed to an upward slope across from them. Near its bottom was an indentation that looked like a scoop had been taken out of the side of the mountain. In its center set a cabin and several other buildings. From this distance, they looked very tiny.

"But how are we going to get there?" Jill looked at the steep, rocky incline below them.

"Don't worry. Mules are surefooted and old Jake has made this trip more times than you can count."

Their decent was slow and tedious. Each time the mule took a step, Jill pictured its foot slipping off one of the boulder's jagged edges protruding from the snow. She held her breath, afraid the mule would lose its footing and they would go tumbling to the rocks below.

At the bottom, a creek flowed. Apparently, a spring was keeping it from freezing. Icicles hung from the rocks lining its bank and a fallen tree created a bridge from one side to the other.

The mule, sensing it was near home, picked up its pace and splashed into the water. Tanner dropped the reins and crossed the creek on the fallen log. After crossing the water, they trekked up a steep incline following a path leading to the cabin, an outhouse and two other small buildings. A picket-type fence made of pointed rough boards surrounded an area Jill assumed was a garden. A large, leafless oak tree stood sentinel in front of the cabin, while a host of other trees surrounded it on all three sides, giving the impression of it being a fortress where intruders could be readily seen before they got to it.

Tanner untied the ropes and gently took Jill off the mule. Snow scrunched loudly under his boots as he walked up the porch steps. When they reached the door he bent down so Jill could lift the latch. Hinges squeaked noisily when Tanner stuck his toe in the crack of the open door and pulled it open.

"Ahhh," he said, "Home, sweet home, at last."

Although it wasn't Jill's own cozy home, she was glad to be there. She was tired and her leg was hurting, actually her whole body hurt. Straw crackled as Tanner laid her on the mattress of a large wood-framed bed. He rummaged around in an old trunk at the foot of the bed, finally pulling out two of the most beautiful quilts Jill had ever seen. She recognized the wedding ring pattern of the first one he spread over her, but the second was unfamiliar. "Do you know what pattern this is?" she questioned as she ran her hand over blocks designed of red fabric with yellow print. Contrasting white blocks quilted with wreaths and crosshatched lines nestled between the red and yellow blocks.

"I believe Stella called it Turkey Tracks," Tanner answered as his finger outlined pieces shaped to resemble the footprint of a turkey. "She said it used to be called Wandering Foot. There was an old superstition that anyone who slept under it would develop wanderlust and a tendency toward a discontented, unstable, roving disposition. In an effort to dispel the curse, but save the pattern, it was renamed Turkey Tracks." In a voice Jill could barely hear, he turned away from her and walked over to the fireplace as he added, "Apparently my grandmother slept under it before it was renamed."

"What?"

"Never mind the details. It should keep you warm until I get some heat in here." He knelt down by the fireplace made of rocks and red clay, laid in wood and kindling, and held a match to it. Soon flames were jumping up and down and smoke rolled up the chimney. He turned as he spoke, "I'm going to..." Jill was already sleeping. Tanner quietly took a pail and went out to the well for water.

When he returned he filled an iron pot and set it in one corner of the fireplace. He carefully removed his torn coat and shirt. The claw marks had begun to redden and he knew if he didn't get something on them soon they would become infected. The mountain people had no doctors, nor did they have any use for any. They claimed their home remedies were as good, if not better, than anything a doctor would give them. In the three years he had been on the mountain, Tanner studied their methods and was increasingly surprised to discover they actually worked as well as anything produced by modern medicine. The only time they were in trouble was when something serious happened and even then, they had their way of dealing with it. In the case of a broken bone, they simply put splints on each side and plastered it up with a mixture of red clay and water and let nature take its course, sometimes they were left with a slight limp if the bone didn't heal right.

He removed the cap from the kerosene lamp which was standing on the table and poured some of the kerosene in a bowl, added sugar to it and stirred the mixture. He knew it was going to burn like fire when he poured the mountaineers' remedy for inflammation on his open wounds. He sat staring at the bowl thinking about what the reaction of the doctors at the hospital in Knoxville would be if they saw him using such unorthodox methods. They would be appalled that he, with all of his training and expertise, would resort to such a "barbaric" treatment of wounds. He picked up the bowl and quickly poured the liquid on the raw flesh of his shoulders.

A gasp woke Jill. She looked over at Tanner. He was sitting in a chair facing the fireplace, his body rigid, large muscles bulging from the sides of his neck and back. A light-yellow liquid trickled over deep red gouges in the flesh on his shoulders and down to the waistband of his buckskin pants.

"What are you doing?" Jill asked.

Her voice surprised Tanner. "Just doctoring up my wounds." He got up from his chair and came toward her.

She held her breath as she watched him move. Curly, reddish-blonde hair covered his upper torso from shoulder to shoulder. Embarrassed to think Tanner might catch her starring at his chest, Jill quickly moved her gaze to his face.

"You missed one by your eye." Dried blood still remained on his face and the slash of the open wound gave him a sinister look. A scar would more than likely be left even after the injury healed.

"I'll get it later. Right now I think we'd better get your leg fixed. I'm going to have to take the cast off, re-set your leg and put on a new cast. Think you're up to it? It's going to hurt like crazy."

"I don't have much choice, do I? Are you sure you know what you're doing? How do you know how to set a leg?"

Tanner knew the questions would begin sooner or later. His life was his business and he didn't want to have to explain himself to yet another person. "It doesn't matter how I know, just count yourself blessed that I do."

He grabbed up a shirt hanging from a peg on the wall, gingerly slipped it on, and went about the business of gathering up the needed supplies to put on a new cast. Out of a clay pot on a shelf covered with numerous other pots, he drew a root shaped like the body of a small man and broke off one of the legs.

"Chew on this while I take off this cast," he commanded as he pushed up her baggy pant leg, retrieved a large tool that looked like a cross between a scissors and a monkey wrench from a black bag and began to snip the cast.

"What is this?" She smelled the root, then tentatively put it to her tongue to see if it had a taste.

"Ginseng."

"But I thought ginseng is used as a…stimulant." What were this man's intentions? He wouldn't be trying to take advantage of her, would he? She held the small piece of root in her fingers, waiting for his answer.

"That's what the Asiatic ginseng is noted for. The ancient medical book of India, *The Atherva Veda*, states ginseng aids the female to bring forth a son, or something like that."

Tanner watched Jill's face for the reaction he knew would come. He also knew he shouldn't tease her, but she took everything so seriously it was fun to try and get her to laugh at her own gullibility.

"Well, I'm *not* going to eat this thing." Jill shoved the root at him, but he ignored her outstretched hand and kept working on the cast.

Trying to hide the grin on his face, Tanner replied, "I didn't give it to you with idea of using it as a love potion, though the idea does sound intriguing, and I have been alone for a long time…" He peaked at her face out of the corner of his eye. Her horrified look made the teasing worthwhile. Now he would tell her the real reason for giving her the ginseng. "The truth is… the kind growing here is used more for medicinal purposes. It has sleep producing qualities and I figured it would help ease the pain for you."

Jill didn't know what to make of this man. He said things so seriously sometimes she really believed he meant them, then he'd laugh, as if she should have understood from the beginning he was only teasing her. She jammed the root into her mouth and chewed, hoping it would put her to sleep until her leg was completely healed and she could leave this place, and this infuriating man, without a back ward glance.

CHAPTER 9

She had fallen asleep and now, upon waking, realized she must have slept for quite a while. Tanner was nowhere to be seen. Jill wondered where he had gone and hoped he would be back soon.

The ginseng hadn't helped ease the pain when Jill's leg was re-set, but she got through it. Now she had a new cast on her leg. She had watched Tanner put it on and marveled at how he seemed to know exactly what to do, but when questioned about it, again he gave vague answers.

Dusk was settling in. The inside of the cabin was shadowy, making it difficult to see clearly. It looked as if the cabin had only one room, the whole of which was no larger than the living room in her house. A fire was burning in the fireplace, casting a glow on what little furniture was in the room. A wooden table and chairs filled the center of the room and a high-backed rocker sat beneath a window.

There were bookshelves on the wall beyond the foot of the

bed, but it was too dark in the room for Jill to make out their titles. Plank shelves, lined with various sizes of pottery jars and cooking utensils, hung above a counter built trestle style.

The squeaking door announced Tanner's entry. Jill saw he hadn't cleaned the cut on his face, dried blood still clung to it. He walked to the fireplace, used a poker to stir the fire, and added two logs. Quietly he approached her, as if he was trying to decide if she was asleep or awake.

Jill said nothing, only watched closely the man coming toward her. He stood over six feet tall with shoulders spanning three-fourths of the width of the doorway he just came through. Most large men Jill had known lumbered across a room, but not this one, this one moved with the grace of the buck deer whose hides he wore for clothing.

"You awake?" Dumb question, Tanner thought as he looked into her wide-open dark eyes.

"Yes."

"Are you hungry? While you were sleeping I went back after the mountain lion and made some stew. It should be about done."

"You made stew out of the cat? And you want me to eat it? You can't be serious!"

"No, I didn't really make a stew out of it, I was only kidding. It's…" Tanner remembered how she ate the rabbit he cooked in the cave without complaining or making the usual crunched up face, "rabbit."

"Are you sure? You hesitated a long time before you said it was rabbit."

"I'm sure." Tanner smiled mischievously at her as he turned and lit the lantern which was in the center of the table, then hung his coat on the peg near the door. With a small iron shovel he dug a cast iron Dutch oven from beneath hot coals in the fireplace and removed the lid, letting the taste-tempting aroma fill the room while he got bowls and spoons down from the shelf.

Tanner set the bowls filled with stew on the table to cool while he propped Jill up with several fat feather-filled pillows. After this morning's experience with the oatmeal, he had no intention of trying to feed her. He removed a brown jug from a snow-filled pail he had brought in earlier, poured some of the liquid in a cup and handed it to Jill along with the bowl of stew.

Jill carefully balanced the bowl on her legs and drank some of the liquid from the cup. "What is this? It tastes like milk, but different."

"It is milk—goat's milk. Drink it, it's good for you. It will help your leg heal faster."

"So you have a nanny goat and a mule. What else?" Jill tried to keep the conversation going while she cleaned up the contents of the bowl. She recognized the potatoes and carrots, but was unsure about the rest of the things in the stew. It was good, so it didn't really matter. She tried not to think of the dead mountain lion as she lifted a bite of meat to her mouth.

"A couple of kids," Tanner answered.

She choked. "Kids? You have children up here with you?"

Tanner laughed as he took her empty bowl and cup. "No, not children, kids—baby goats. Do you want some more stew?"

"No thanks. It was very good. So are you totally self-sufficient up here by yourself?"

"Pretty much. In the summer I raise a garden and store food for the winter and I hunt for my meat. Don't need much more. Whatever else I need I get from the Tuttle clan or by doing some fur trading. I trade for coffee, one of the things I seemed to have acquired an addiction to and can't resist buying. The sassafras tea the mountaineers drink is okay, but just not the same as a good cup of coffee. I get a bolt of cotton fabric every once in a while for the Tuttle women to repay them for all they do for me. There have been a lot of times I've come back from hunting to find a pie or bread or something else they've cooked setting on my table."

Tanner thought about all the times Julie Ann sneaked off and brought him some special dish she prepared for him. Her pa would have taken a willow switch to her backside if he had caught her, no matter that she was twenty years old. Julie Ann tried everything she could think of to entice him into becoming her husband. But Tanner wasn't interested in Julie Ann, or any other woman, at least he hadn't been until now.

"But doesn't it get lonely, being here by yourself all of the time?" A few days of being alone had been all right, but Jill couldn't imagine what it would be like for years. Maybelle said she had known Tanner for three years. *Had he been alone all that time or had a woman come to the mountains with him? If so, what happened to her? Where did he come from?*

"It did at first, but then I met the Tuttle clan. Tanner smiled as he told Jill about his first encounter with W.H.

He had been hunting since early morning and only had a few rabbits to show for the whole day. It was almost dusk when he sat down on an old log near the creek for a short rest before heading back to his cabin. Suddenly he heard a noise coming from the trees near him. He raised the gun to his shoulder and waited until the large buck was within shooting range. Another shot rang out at the same time. The deer fell to the ground. Tanner watched the wizened face and body of a short old man appear from the same part of the woods where the deer had come.

The old man pointed his gun straight at Tanner's heart and

with glaring eyes yelled, "Ya almost killed me, ya blasted fool. What 'n the name of up yonder are ya' doin' on my huntin' grounds? I been hunting this area for neigh onta sixty-five years and ain't nobody bothered it afore. Dang fereigners, anyways."

"I'm sorry. I didn't know you were there. And I'm not exactly a foreigner. My grandpa, Gus Tanner, was born and died a mountaineer. He lived over in Pine Hollow."

The old man spread his thumb and fingers across his jaw and ran them down across a sparse beard, as if trying to remember Tanner's grandfather. "Yep, I recollect old man Tanner. Rest o' his kin was from up Blue Mountain way. Seems he was shunned by 'em when he up and married a city gal and brung her up here. If I remember right, she stayed long enough to let their son get a couple of years old, then beat it back ta where she come from. Thet boy be yer pa then?"

"Yes, he was." Tanner was relieved when the old man lowered his gun, but he stayed cautious just the same. In the two weeks he'd been on the mountain this was the first person he had seen. He had been warned the mountaineers didn't take too kindly to strangers. His only hope was that since his grandfather was from the mountains, these people would accept him. After all, he wasn't going to bother them; he only wanted to be alone.

"Help me git this deer on my mule so's I kin git home afore dark or Ma'll be havin' a conniption." The old man led a mule out from behind the trees and as Tanner helped him hoist the deer onto its back and lash it on, he asked, "Where's yer mule?"

"I don't have one."

"Well, how was ya gonna git a deer ta yer place?"

"I don't know. I hadn't thought that far yet."

The old man looked Tanner square in the eye and shook his head. "Youngins! Ain't none o' ya got enough smoke curlin' from yer chimneys. Come along with me."

Tanner didn't question the fact the old man wanted him to come home with him. It would be a chance to find out what his grandfather's people were really like. His father brought him to the mountain to visit Grandpa only twice that Tanner could remember, and then only for a day. Even as a child Tanner had been impressed by the way Grandpa lived totally without need of anyone else.

They walked for almost an hour before they came to a large clearing lined with cabins of differing sizes and shapes. Shoeless children ran about playing a robust game of tag. A crowd of men and teenage boys began to trail them, commenting on the size of the deer W.H. bagged, and looking Tanner over with unhidden curiosity.

They stopped in front of a cabin which looked as if the original house had been added to several times. A large woman burst out of the door. "Well, old man, looks like yer got yerself a dandy buck." She slapped him on the back and then cupped her hands around her mouth and set off with a chain of "oo-e's" bringing all the women out from their cabins.

"Yep, I shore did. This here is Gus Tanner's grandson. And this here's Stella, head of the clan."

Stella put her hands on her ample hips and declared, "Now, W.H., ya knows yer the head of the clan. Why ya gotta talk like yer mind went a ramblin' like wild geese flyin' west? I'm jest yer wife, nothin' more."

"Humph." Old W.H. mumbled as he walked up on the porch, sat in an old rocking chair, closed his eyes and rocked slowly back and forth.

Tanner turned to Stella, "Well, guess I better get going."

"Nonsense. Ya kin stay fer some vittles and a night's rest afore ya head home. Now sit yerself down. We'll be havin' some fresh venison soon. What's yer given name, son?"

"David, but my friends just call me Tanner."

Tanner sat in the rocking chair next to W.H., who appeared to be sleeping, and watched what was happening. The deer was hung by its hind legs to a hefty tree branch, the hide removed and steaks cut from it. A large fire pit smoldered at one end of the clearing, to it pieces of dried hickory were added. A Paul-Bunyan-size, cast iron frying pan filled with floured deer steaks was put on a grate over the fire. Whole potatoes and ears of corn still in their husks were also laid on the grate.

With his eyes still closed, W.H. suddenly started talking. "My pa and me claimed thet huntin' spot as ours when I was no bigger than a pup. Back when Russian wild hogs were still plentiful. I remember how the men would be huntin' them whilst the women got a fire goin' fer rendering the lard. We'd cut up the hog, cover each piece with lard, pack it into a gunny sack and tie it to the side of the mule fer totin' home. Ma made cracklin' bread from the renderin's thet melted in yer mouth. We still go huntin' them, but there ain't many 'round no more." He still hadn't opened his eyes, he seemed finished, then suddenly started talking again. "Listen to the mule, boy. He'll always tell ya what he's gonna do afore he does it."

Tanner waited for him to explain what that meant, but he never did and moments later soft snores were coming from the old man.

Several sets of saw horses were set up with planks laid across them. The women draped dish towels over them then carried numerous bowls of coleslaw, baked beans, succotash and freshly churned butter out of their homes as well as plates and silverware. The deer meat, potatoes and sweet corn were added to the makeshift tables and all were called to the feast.

After supper the women cleaned up dishes and put away what little was left of the food. The men pulled out fiddles, banjos and guitars. Soon rousing jigs were being danced and there was a whole lot of foot-stomping and hand-clapping going on to the beat of the music. Several women, young and old, pulled Tanner out and whirled around with him on the dirt dance floor.

Some youngsters grabbed empty canning jars and began blowing over the opening to create a sad, mourning sound as they joined the musicians in a soft ballad about Tom Dooley, who killed poor Laura Foster and now he was about to die for his crime.

After the music died down and everything had been put away, he was directed by Stella to sleep in the barn. He suspected she was being cautious about him. Mountaineers were basically very open to strangers, but the last few years had brought them a lot of trouble from outsiders.

The next morning as he was about to leave, W.H. handed the reins of a mule he was currying to Tanner. “He’s yers. Name’s Jake. Jest remember what I told ya ‘bout listenin’ to the mule and you’ll git along jest fine.”

“But I can’t take one of your mules,” Tanner protested.

“I owed yer grandpa a favor I ne’er did git paid. Now it’s done. Git along with ya now and don’t let me catch ya messin’ ‘round my huntin’ spot agin.”

Tanner finished telling Jill the story of how he met the Tuttle clan, adding that Ned is the son of W.H. and Stella and there are forty-three members of the clan, counting aunts, uncles and cousins, living in the clearing.

“You know, it’s a good thing I took old W.H.’s advice and listened to the mule or I wouldn’t have found you.”

“What do you mean?” Jill found the story of the Tuttles interesting, but the part about the mule made no sense at all.

“I was trying to get Jake to turn back and head toward the cabin, but, being the stubborn mule that he is, he kept moving straight on. I let him have his way and in a little while he came to a complete stop and refused to move at all. That's when I spotted you laying by the tree. You were almost totally covered with snow. At first I thought you were dead." Tanner scanned the beautiful face before him. "I'm glad you aren't," he said softly as he began to take off his shirt.

CHAPTER 10

"What are you doing?" Jill watched as Tanner peeled off his shirt. Her heart pounded as she tried to figure out how to defend herself. There were a number of reasons not to let her guard down and get involved with this man. Her mind clicked off a fast list of what those might be. First of all, there was no future in becoming involved with Tanner. His life was here and she had responsibilities at home, a child and a business to run. Second, she knew nothing about him. She didn't know where he came from, anything about his family, but most of all she didn't know why he was hiding out in the mountains. Third, was not wanting to become physically involved with a man unless she was married to him. She still had her religious convictions, even if she wasn't sure anymore if God really cared about what she would or wouldn't do. There had been no one in her life since Tom died who made it necessary to even think about such things, but now, because of her attraction to Tanner, she needed to. The last thing she wanted was to get home and discover that she had gotten involved with a man whose picture graced the post office walls on a WANTED poster.

Tanner saw the way Jill's wide eyes stared at his bare chest, then quickly looked away, as if she were embarrassed to be caught looking at him.

"I'm only going to clean up these wounds, don't get nervous."

"I'm not *nervous*." She watched as Tanner took some kind of root from one of the pottery jars and crushed it into a fine powder. He put some of the powder in a bowl and some in a cup and set them on the table. From a teakettle hanging over the fire, he filled the cup with hot water, stirred it and handed it to Jill.

"Here, drink this," he commanded as he added a few drops of hot water to the bowl and mixed it to form a sticky mucilaginous mass. He poured water on a cloth and cleaned the dried blood from the cut near his eye, then dipped the cloth in the gel-like substance and began to apply it to the deep scratches..

"What is this?" Jill asked as she stared at the liquid in the cup Tanner gave to her. It seemed she was constantly asking the same question about things he gave her to eat or drink.

"Comfrey, also called knitbone. It contains allantoin, a cell proliferant, which increases the speed at which a wound or broken bone can heal. It also helps asthma, ulcers…" Tanner stopped suddenly, realizing he had piqued Jill's curiosity even more by going into a detailed description of the medicinal properties of comfrey. He had to do something to get her mind focused on something else. "Would you mind putting some of this on the scratches on my back? I can't reach them very well."

Tanner handed her the bowl, then straddled the chair backwards, his chest resting against the chair back with his back to her. Light blonde hair curled thickly over his shoulder blades then turned baby-fine as it made its way over the expanse of his ribs. Four parallel lines of angry looking red claw marks marred the flesh in various spots on his back. Jill took the cloth, dipped it into the bowl, and gently touched it to the beginning of one set of the marks. When Tanner didn't flinch or react in any way, she continued dipping the cloth into the gelled comfrey and applying it to the wounds. Her hand gently pushed his long hair away and held it aside as she doctored the scratches running down the side of his neck.

Tanner groaned inwardly. It had been a long time since he had felt the touch of another human being. He needed to make her stop but he couldn't, not yet. Instead he prayed for control over the feelings washing over him.

Thoughts of Emily intruded. Before she had gotten sick her greatest desire was to have lots of money and the prestige it would bring. He wanted children; she wanted a mansion in the elite part of town. Until Tim's death, she got what she wanted. His brother's last few words of "be happy, Tanner" jolted him into thinking about his life, about what he wanted and didn't want, and how unhappy he really was. He had gone searching for some kind of meaning for his life. He found the Lord and came to understand the only way to true happiness was through belief in Jesus.

"Tanner?" Jill had finished putting the comfrey on his back a few minutes ago, but Tanner hadn't moved, nor said a word. He sat stark still staring into the fire. "Tanner. Where are you?"

"Oh, sorry. I guess my mind wandered off for a while. Thanks for doctoring me up." He put his shirt back on and got up.

Jill was disappointed. He had not reacted to her touch at all. She wanted him to take her in his arms and tell her she was desirable. But what she wanted, and what she would allow herself to have, were two totally different things. She supposed the need to be wanted came from having been rejected by her own husband.

Tanner quickly moved to place several large logs in the fireplace. He stared at flames jumping from the burning wood. *You're going to have to stay as far away as possible from her, she is way too tempting.* He gathered another quilt and pillow from the large trunk, blew out the lantern and laid down on the hard wood floor fully clothed.

"Good-night, Jill."

"Good-night." Jill wrestled with the covers, trying to get comfortable. The cast was awkward and her leg ached. From the glow of the fire, she could see Tanner's back moving with each breath he took as he lay on his side, his face away from her. She held her breath until she could match the rhythm of his deep breathing. Soon she felt as if she were being rocked back and forth very slowly and drifted off to sleep.

Morning brought sunshine streaming in through the windows and the chop-chop-chopping sound of an axe as it came in contact with a log. The quilt bed of Tanner's was gone, as was he. Jill assumed he was the one outside chopping wood. Her eyes scanned the room and stopped at the bookshelf on the wall opposite her. Names such as Chaucer, Hemingway and Thoreau stood out from the books' spines. There were well-worn copies of *Old Yeller, Wyatt Earp and Gone With The Wind,* as well as numerous paperback editions of various writers of suspense and intrigue, flanked by thick copies of medical books. Medical books? Now what was a mountain man doing with those?

The creaking door brought Jill's eyes to it. Tanner's arms were loaded with chunks of wood which he dropped into a box near the fireplace.

"Well, I see you're awake. How do you feel this morning?"

"Pretty good, but I'm getting tired of lying in this bed."

"I think you better take it easy yet today. If this sun stays out all day, it may melt the snow enough so we can get you back tomorrow. You were staying at the cabin up on the ridge above where I found you, right?"

"Right. I need to get back so I can take care of….. some things."

Again the question of another man popped into Tanner's mind. He wasn't sure he believed her story of having been all alone. What person in their right mind would come to the mountains by themselves at a time of the year when it's been known to snow for weeks, making it virtually impossible to get anywhere? Granted, the cabins in that area where more modern and some even had telephones, but still…

"Is there a phone there so you can call someone to come and get you?"

"Yes, there is." Jill hadn't thought about not being able to drive her car, now it hit her how difficult even the simplest things were going to be with a cast on her right leg. If it had been her left, she still would have been able to drive. How was she going to get to clients' houses? And if she couldn't, how could she keep her business going? Life seemed to keep making twists and turns around her plans, never quite getting to them. Just when she thought she was almost there, something always happened to wreck it. Would a simple life ever be hers? She doubted it.

They spent the rest of the day quietly, with Jill browsing through some of Tanner's books and taking several naps, while Tanner made a pair of crutches for her.

She woke to the tantalizing smell of meat cooking. In the fireplace, Tanner had placed a tripod with a rack. Thick steaks sizzled as flames licked the juices dripping from them. Yams were pulled from the coals, their skins darkened to within a hair's breadth of being burned. On the table, a jar of fat dill pickles offered vinegary delight as a compliment to the rest of the meal.

As they enjoyed the meal, Jill talked about her interior decorating business and her son. Tanner talked about his life on the mountain and his mountain friends, but when Jill questioned him about his family or his life before coming to the mountain, he would only say, "None of it matters," and smoothly change the subject.

Each of them thought about the attraction they felt for each other, and what could have been had they met at another time, another place, but neither voiced their thoughts. Instead they were careful not to touch, and not to look into each other's eyes.

CHAPTER 11

Jill leaned on the new crutches Tanner made her and looked out the window. It must be late morning, but since there were no clocks, Jill couldn't be certain. At first it had driven her crazy not knowing what time it was, she had lived by the clock for so long it seemed like a part of her was missing. But there was no need to know here, time just melted away slowly. Like snow melting away from the heat of the sun, leaving small patches of brown grass flickering in the breeze.

She watched the taut muscles of Tanner's lean body as he swung the axe high above his head, then down to meet a large piece of wood, breaking it into smaller pieces. Again and again, he repeated the same actions, never letting up, as if there were a demon after him and he couldn't stop or he would be caught by it. He spent all morning outside, away from her, except for the one time when he brought in a piece of meat and laid it on the counter. It was just as well he stayed away, his nearness caused a fluttery feeling inside her she didn't want to acknowledge.

She looked at the meat on the counter. Side pork, he called

it, from a Russian wild hog. Well, the least she could do was fix them something to eat as her way of thanking him for all he had done for her. He was taking her back to the cabin this afternoon so there wouldn't be another chance.

Jill hobbled over to the counter and found some potatoes tucked down under in a metal pail. Once they were peeled and sliced she reached up to get the crock of lard from the shelf, her crutches crashed to the floor. Simple things were made so much more difficult having to depend on the crutches to get around. She was really beginning to appreciate the problems handicapped people encountered on a daily basis. The frying pan was hanging on a nail by the fireplace. How she was going to get the potatoes and meat over to the fireplace was a problem since moving required both hands on the crutches.

A further search of the shelves turned up a burlap bag she used to carry the meat and potatoes to the fireplace. Finally, she was all set. She would fry the meat, take it out of the pan and put in the potatoes and cook them. She had never cooked in a fireplace before, other than roasting a few marshmallows, but it couldn't be that difficult. She had watched Tanner do it; she'd just do it the same way.

She stirred the coals, making a nice hot bed on which she laid a couple of pieces of very dry-looking wood. Clay bricks stuck up from the ashes on both sides of the smoldering wood on which Jill placed the metal grate that stood by the fireplace wall. Next she put a large spoonful of lard in the frying pan and set the pan on the grate. Slowly the lard melted. She added the meat to the pan and waited for it to begin cooking. It didn't seem to be doing anything. She took a fork and turned the thickly sliced strips over. It hadn't cooked at all. What she needed was a hotter fire. She reached into the firewood box and found some smaller pieces of wood and dry bark and stuffed them in under the grate. Flames began dancing on the bottom of the pan as the kindling caught fire.

Satisfied that she had the meat cooking now, she hobbled back to the wooden counter to clean up. The sound of rapidly spitting grease hitting the burning wood with a pizz, pizz, pizz caused Jill to turn and look at the meat-filled pan. It was on fire! Flames were jumping out of the pan; sparks flew to the floor and into the wood box, catching it on fire, too. Smoke was filling the cabin.

The door burst open. "What is…?" Without another word Tanner picked Jill up and carried her outside, dropping her to the ground and running back into the cabin. Using the water bucket, he drenched the wood box, grasped the frying pan handle, carried it through the open door to the porch and threw pan, burning meat and all, out into a snow drift.

He glared at Jill as she sat shivering in the cold snow near where he had thrown the pan. She watched him turn and storm back into the cabin. Smoke billowed out of the door as it was chased by a snapping blanket, disappearing as the wind lifted it and carried it away.

With her left knee raised and her arms folded over it, Jill laid her forehead on her arms and sobbed. She felt a blanket being put over her shoulders, but she didn't move. She couldn't stop crying. It was as if the dam she built to keep her emotions under control burst. All the pain, of Tom's death, his and her father's infidelity, having to move out of her home and fighting to keep her business going came crashing in on her.

Tanner wrapped his arms around Jill's shoulders and pulled her to him. She hadn't stopped shaking, nor did she look at him, she only hid her face in his chest and wept. He carried her back inside and, with her still in his arms, sat down on a chair and waited for the tears to subside. He'd been scared when he first saw smoke rolling out from under the roof, then furious when he discovered Jill caused it by having too hot of a fire under the greasy meat. Now he was calm, he even felt sorry for her.

"M-must be t-this broken l-leg making m-me act so s-stupid," Jill said between hiccups as she raised her tear-stained face to Tanner's.

"It's okay. No real harm done, it's just a little smoky in here, that's all." Tanner's consoling hand stroked down her hair like he was petting a cat.

"Davey?"

Tanner turned his head to see Toby's ash-white face looking in through the open door.

"Toby, what's the matter?" Tanner knew it had to be something serious from the look on the boy's face.

"It's Ma. The granny's been with her since early this morn and the baby ain't come yet. Pa sent me after you."

Tanner got up and set Jill on the chair. "I've got to go. I'll be back as soon as I can." He whisked a black bag from beneath the high bed and disappeared through the door, closing it behind him.

Jill limped over to the window and watched the large man and a small boy ride away on twin mules. All kinds of questions plagued her. Would Maybelle and her baby survive? How could Tanner help? And what was in the bag he had taken with him? How long before he would be back?

She spent part of the afternoon cleaning up the mess her fire made, careful not to use all of what little water was left in the bucket. She laid the wet wood from the wood box out on the plank floor in front of the fireplace hoping it would dry soon. The wood in the fireplace had burned down to a half-dozen baseball size chunks. Hunger prompted her to try cooking over the fire once more, but this time she used little grease and carefully watched the potatoes as they fried. She ate them from the pan when they cooled and marveled at how different food tasted when cooked over a wood fire instead of on a stove.

The fire died down and the damp piece she put on it sizzled, but didn't seem to be burning. The cabin began to feel chilly. Jill contemplated trying to go outside and get wood from the pile Tanner created earlier in the day, but vetoed the idea when she thought about trying to navigate the steps and slippery snow with crutches. She decided to curl up under the quilts on the bed to keep warm while she waited for Tanner to return.

The room was totally dark when Jill opened her eyes. She knew she should get up and light the lantern, but the room was cold and it was warmer under the covers. A sound came from over by the door. Jill's body stiffened with fear. Something, or someone, was in the cabin with her. The crutches she left propped up by the table crashed to the floor. "Tanner?" she whispered. No answer came. She lay huddled beneath the blankets, waiting. For what, she didn't know. She heard no more noises and after what seemed like an endless amount of time, she talked herself into believing there was nothing in the room with her, the crutches must have slipped to the floor of their own accord.

Slipping off the bed, Jill grabbed the back of a wooden chair. Several pushes and hops later she managed to complete the distance across the small room and reach the table, where she lit the lamp. She looked around the room and saw nothing. Then, suddenly, something moved above her head. Jill raised her eyes and saw a squirrel sitting on one of the rafters, its tail whisked back and forth like a frothy fern being used for a fan. It chattered at her as if *she* were the intruder. How she was going to get the critter out of the cabin didn't matter right now, she needed to get a fire going before she froze to death.

There were only a few warm ashes left in the fireplace, not enough to start logs on fire, she was sure. She needed to find some paper or something she could use to get a good flame going. Nothing was visible. She moved to the trunk at the foot of the bed and opened it. The heavy quilts of colored wool Tanner used for a bed were on top, she lifted them out. Beneath was a gold-framed picture of a young woman. Jill carried it over to the light of the lantern so she could get a better look. The woman had medium length blonde hair styled in a classic wedge cut that complemented her perfectly oval face. Her large green eyes sparkled, her flawless skin glowed and her scoop-necked dress revealed not one freckle or mole. Jill thought of the ugly, brown, pea-size mole that stood out just below her collar bone. It was the reason she never wore low necklines and why she felt self-conscious even wearing a bathing suit. She asked her doctor once about having it removed, but he told her that it was harmless and called it a "beauty mark". Funny, it didn't make her feel beautiful.

She laid the picture on the table and went back to check the rest of the contents of the trunk. She knew she wasn't going to find anything to burn in there, but now her curiosity had the upper hand.

There were other pictures in the trunk. One of a distinguished-looking man with the same sapphire colored eyes as Tanner's and a pretty woman with short blonde hair. It was easy to see these two were his parents. Another of two young boys with their arms around each other's shoulders, one taller and more slender than the other, otherwise they could have been twins. A fourth photo showed a man and woman in their late twenties or early thirties and three children whose ages ranged from about three to seven, two boys and a girl. Next she withdrew a wooden plaque imprinted with *The Oath of Hippocrates* and a deep walnut-colored frame that held a medical degree for David Patrick Tanner from the University of Tennessee. So Tanner is a doctor! Then what in the world is he doing living like a recluse on this mountain, Jill wondered.

She hadn't found anything to burn, except maybe Tanner's ears for not telling her the truth. She returned all the pictures and his degree to the trunk. Taking a sharp knife, she whittled one of the pieces of wood until she had a small pile of wood chips to use for starting the fire.

After getting the fire going, Jill decided to try and chase the chattering squirrel from the rafters and out of the cabin. She opened the door and faced the fiercely piercing stare of two deep set eyes. Startled, she sucked in her breath and held it until she realized the eyes belonged to a large owl sitting on the branch of a small tree in front of the porch. The scratching noise of the squirrel's toenails on the plank floor informed her of the small animal's departure as its fanning tail brushed across her leg and it streaked off the porch. The owl let off a series of hoo, hoo, hoo's and flew after the squirrel.

Jill closed the door and collapsed in a chair near the fireplace. She sat mesmerized by the flames and lost in thought about the man who called this cabin home. What happened to make him quit practicing medicine? But he hadn't really quit, he fixed Jill's broken leg and now he was delivering Maybelle's baby. Maybe he's dedicated his life to being a doctor for the mountain people. But if that were so, he would have said right off that he was a doctor. No, there was more to it, and Jill intended to find out what he was hiding, and why, when he returned. Another thing she intended to ask about was the beautiful woman in the picture.

Jill laid Tanner's bedding out on the floor and crawled back into bed. She left the lantern on so he could find his way without having to stumble around in the dark. Silence surrounded her, peacefulness flowed through her, and she wished she could stay right where she was forever.

CHAPTER 12

Morning came, but there were no signs of Tanner having been there at all during the night.

The blankets Jill put out for him still laid in exactly the same position. Once again the cabin was cold. Jill forced herself to get out of bed, swing to the fireplace on her crutches and rebuild the fire. She hadn't realized how convenient a furnace was until now.

Jill's stomach growled. She searched the shelves for something to eat and found what she needed to make pancakes. She surprised herself at how good she was getting at cooking over an open fire, especially after her first disaster.

With pancakes piled high on a plate, Jill sat down at the table. She put two on her plate and spread home-churned butter and clover honey over them. Just as she was about to put a bite in her mouth the cabin door opened.

Tanner was back. He looked tired and rumpled, but smiled at Jill as he grabbed a plate and piled pancakes on it.

"Looks like you learned how to cook while I was gone."

Tanner put a large bite in his mouth. “Mm-m, these are really good.”

Indignant at his assumption she didn’t know how to cook, Jill answered him, “You don’t need to act so surprised. I do know how to cook, just not in such a primitive way.” Remembering why Tanner had been gone, she questioned hesitantly, “How are Maybelle and the baby?”

“They’re doing fine now.” Tanner looked at Jill, she seemed genuinely concerned. It would be nice to be able to talk to someone about the difficult breech birth he had just been through. There was a length of time when he hadn’t been sure if the baby or Maybelle would live.

“I know you’re a doctor, Tanner. I should have been able to figure it out before, but I didn’t put it all together until I saw your medical degree in the trunk. Why didn’t you tell me?”

Tanner was furious. All he wanted was to be left alone, to live his life as he saw fit. Every time he went back home, everyone tried to get him to “be reasonable” and come back to the city. They thought he was wasting his life living here in the mountains and should be back home practicing medicine with his father in his prestigious practice. If he had been, both Maybelle and the baby would be dead right now. But no one seemed to understand or care about these mountaineers. And he wasn’t just helping them, he was learning, learning about the medicinal powers of plants growing in the wild. Someday he would be able to help people who had no way of getting prescription drugs, but could, instead, grow their own medicine.

Now here was yet another person who would probably tell him he was crazy. Someone he learned to care for very deeply in the few days they had been together. She seemed different from the people he had been around all his life, but he still wasn’t ready to risk being open and honest with her. He already had enough people laughing at him, his way of life, and his dream.

"Because it was none of your business. Now let's get going and get you back where you belong."

Tanner shoved a blanket, some jerky, and various other things into a pair of side packs and flung them over his shoulder. He practically ripped the door off its hinges when he yanked it open.

"I'll wait outside while you get dressed." Tanner's steel blue eyes scanned Jill's shirt-clad-only body before he walked out; slamming the door behind him so hard it shook the pottery jars standing precariously close to the edges of the two shelves near the door.

"How childish," Jill muttered as she again put on the same clothes she had worn for three days. It would feel good to get home. She glanced around the room. Their unfinished breakfast still sat on the table, smoke curled up the chimney from the burning logs in the fireplace, a book of Thoreau's journal entries at Waldon's Pond Jill had been reading lay on the brightly quilted bed. She remembered the passage about never having a companion as companionable as solitude and had to agree. When she read it, she thought Tanner must have underlined it as a statement of his own feelings. She thought about how lonely she felt this past year even though she was surrounded constantly by people. These days spent in the mountains had been quiet and very peaceful. She felt refreshed, and a little sad to be leaving.

Jill put on her coat, pulled on the hat and mittens Maybelle had given her to wear, and wished she could stay long enough to hold a new baby in her arms once more. Knowing it would only be other women's babies she would hold from now on created an actual physical ache in her arms. Her dreams of a houseful of children died with Tom. The only other man she felt a deep attraction for stood outside, waiting to take her back and be rid of her, waiting to resume his peaceful life of solitude. She picked up the crutches Tanner made for her, ran her hand down the smooth surface of the wood and hobbled out the door and onto the porch.

Tanner picked her up in his arms and carried her to the mule, tied her crutches on and slid in behind her on the saddle.

They traveled in silence. Tanner had shortened the stirrups to fit the length of Jill's legs. His arm was wrapped around her, holding her close to him. Jill wanted to lean her head back against his chest, feel his chin rest on the top of her head, but instead she kept her upper body rigid and tried to concentrate on something other than his closeness.

Thick gray clouds rolled slowly across the sky. Pine trees seemingly surrounded them, showing a break in their thickness only when you were right next to it. Heavy clumps of snow stuck to their branches and bowed them toward the ground. Only animal tracks broke the surface of the untouched white velvet that lay in arched drifts, bubbles and swirls before them. In the distance, a white-tailed deer stood chewing on the bark of a small tree, its antlers circling high above its head like a crown. As they neared the deer, its head raised, its tail stood straight up, then it ran swiftly into the thick woods.

Jill broke the silence. "It sure is beautiful up here."

"What?" Tanner hadn't heard what Jill said to him, he was too wrapped up in thoughts of how much he was going to miss her when she was gone.

"I said it's beautiful up here."

"Yes, it is." Tanner was able to reply. He wasn't sure if this overwhelming need to hold her was from such a long time of being alone or if it was because this woman seemed so special. Either way, it didn't matter, there could be no future for them; they lived in two different worlds.

"How much longer before we get there?" It seemed as if they had been traveling for days, even though it had only been about an hour. The hardness of the saddle was beginning to make Jill feel uncomfortable and wish she could get down and walk. She laughed at herself for even thinking about walking as she envisioned herself trying to trudge through the knee-deep snow with crutches.

"We should get there a little before noon." A light snow began to fall and Tanner hoped they would get to the cabin long before the storm Ned predicted hit. He probably should have taken Ned's advice and kept her with him a few more days, but she had people at home who were more than likely worried about her. If they could get to the cabin, she could at least call to let them know she was all right. He realized she wasn't used to riding a mule and could probably use a break. "Do you want to stop and rest?"

"That would be nice." In the business world, Jill could ask for what she wanted and needed but in relationships she could not. Her parents taught her that it wasn't nice for girls to be "pushy", that she should wait until she was asked if she wanted something, and Tom reaffirmed the lesson by telling her repeatedly he didn't like demanding women. It irritated her to feel so embarrassed to ask for what she wanted, but it was another of those old behaviors she planned to eliminate. This would be a good time and place to start. "My bottom is getting sore from this saddle and I'm hungry. Didn't I see you put something to eat in the pack?"

"Yes, some jerky. We can stop here for a while, but not too long." Tanner looked up at threatening sky as he got off the mule. He lifted Jill down and stood her next to the mule so she could lean on him for support while he spread a blanket on the snow.

"Looks like we're having a picnic," Jill quipped.

"Yea, right, in the middle of a snow storm." Tanner commented as he scooped Jill into his arms, carried her over and gently set her down on the blanket. He handed her a piece of jerky and the canteen, "Your caviar and champagne, madam."

As Jill's teeth tugged on a piece of beef jerky she looked out on the beauty in front of her. Snow covered trees reminding her of the flocked Christmas trees her father always insisted on. Her parent's relationship always seemed so perfect, granted there had been a few problems, but nothing serious. They always lived by the rule "Never let the sun set on your anger.". How could her father have fooled them all for so long? Was Melissa the only mistress he'd had? She took a deep breath trying to keep away tears threatening to spill.

Tanner wondered what thoughts were going through Jill's mind. She looked so sad. Before he had a chance to think over what he was doing, he wrapped his hand around the back of Jill's neck and pulled her to him. He placed soft flitting kisses across her nose and cheeks, finally landing on her lips. Just as the kiss became passionate, he heard the word "careful" as if it had been whispered in his ear. He withdrew his lips from Jill's and looked around, but saw no one.

CHAPTER 13

Tanner turned in time to see Jill struggling to get up from the blanket. He moved to get to her before she fell, but by the time he got there she was standing, though somewhat unsteadily. He lifted her onto Jake's saddle and took the reins in his hand and stood looking into a face that held no clue as to what she was feeling and said, "I'm sorry, Jill. I shouldn't have…" at the same time as she said, "I'm sorry, but I don't want…"

Neither of them finished what they were saying, but laughed nervously at the fact that they had spoken at the same time.

"Go ahead, finish what you were saying." Tanner needed to know exactly what it was she didn't want.

Jill hesitated. There was no need to tell him what her problem was since nothing had really happened. Nor would it. She would make certain of that. It was just a kiss. Only a little kiss. "No, that's okay. Let's just forget it."

Tanner walked beside the ambling mule wondering if he could forget the way Jill felt in his arms and was saddened by the thought of her leaving.

The snowfall was getting progressively thicker as they slowly made their way down the mountainside. The cabin where they were headed was a little closer to civilization, less rustic. Paved roads lead to the semi-isolated cabins built in this area. They were owned by men with enough money to handle the great expense of building in a remote area, as well as having telephone lines and electricity installed.

Tanner didn't normally come this far down on the mountain, but one of the Tuttle boys told him of seeing a large patch of sassafras shrubs near the cabin where Jill was staying. Sassafras was used by the mountaineers as a blood-builder, and frequently as a diuretic. Tanner intended to dig the roots, take them home and test them for other medical uses when the snow storm hit. He had given up digging the roots and was heading home when he found Jill.

Jill had said very little since their picnic in the snow. She looked so tiny sitting on the back of the large red sorrel mule. Tanner wasn't sure it was a wise idea, but he wanted to be close to her once more. "Mind if I join you?"

"No, I guess not." Having Tanner so close to her again wouldn't be easy, but he had been walking for a long time and Jill was sure he could use the rest. He slid in behind her. The heat of his body radiated into hers as his chest pressed against her back. His hands didn't touch her, instead one held the reins, the other rested on the top of his leg. He made a clicking noise and the mule increased its speed to a gallop. Jill bounced up and down in the saddle.

"Obviously you've never ridden a horse." Tanner moved his arm around her waist and felt the thumping of her body as it came into hard contact with the saddle.

"You mean I don't ride like a real cowgirl? Oh, I'm so disappointed. Actually, I thought I was doing rather well just staying on the back of this massive beast."

Tanner laughed at Jill's wit. Not only was she beautiful and intelligent, but she also had a good sense of humor. He liked that. "Well, what you do is pretend that you are matching the rhythm of your..." Tanner stopped talking as he realized he could no longer use the descriptions of his former life. This Christian walk required talking a whole different language than he had used before. "...dance partner. Only this time your partner is a mule. Just hold your legs close to his body and as the saddle moves back and forth on his back, you move with it. Yea, like that. I think you've got it."

The rest of the ride to the cabin was filled with companionable conversation. Tanner asked questions about Alex, Carrie and Jill's work as an interior decorator. And Jill answered them, not realizing until much later he still hadn't mentioned any of the people whose pictures were in the trunk in his cabin.

"Wow, I can't imagine what the inside of this place must look like," Tanner said as they came near what Jill had nonchalantly called a cabin. The A-frame structure was built of red cedar. A balcony ran across the full length of the upper floor, creating a roof for the front porch supported by round pillars of cedar.

Tanner took Jill off the mule and stood her on the porch. Patches of cinnamon-colored cedar were visible in areas of the porch floor where there was no snow. A six-paned window of curved glass showed various kinds of potted vinery hanging from the ceiling inside.

"You can put Jake over in the shed. I'm going to call home and let everyone know I'm safe and sound while you do that."

Tanner handed Jill the crutches and headed for the large barn-shaped shed she pointed out. It, too, was built of red cedar. He took the saddle and a bedroll, in which he had wrapped clean clothes for himself, off Jake and rubbed him down, talking to the mule as he did so. "Whoever the guy is who owns this place must have a lot of money. Makes me wonder why Jill had to struggle so much, give up her house and everything if she has a *friend* who is so rich. Why hasn't she said anything about him?" He cut the twine from one of the bales of straw stacked neatly in the corner and threw it down on the clean concrete floor for Jake, then tucked the bedroll under his arm and headed for the house.

Once inside, he took off his snow-covered boots and placed them on the rug near where Jill's boots set with beaded water trickling off them. He hung his torn buckskin coat next to one made of white ermine in the spacious coat closet. Tanner ran his hand down its length, feeling the softness of the fur and wondering if all three coats in the closet belonged to Jill. He could hear her voice coming from another room, confirming she would be ready to go home first thing in the morning.

In stocking feet, he ventured into a large open room. Across from where he stood, a rustic looking raised fireplace of reddish-brown stone covered most of the wall from ceiling to floor. In front of it lay a huge black bearskin rug. Its glassy, glaring eyes stared at Tanner, while an open mouth full of sharp teeth threatened to bite if he stepped close. He wandered through the room that could be seen from outside through the huge curved window. It was furnished tastefully in various shades of red and accented with black and white. A long high-backed sofa of softly stuffed red velvet and two matching overstuffed chairs with ottomans filled the room. Two end tables displaying matching antique white lamps with hand-painted red roses on them flanked the sofa. He flipped through coffee table books filled with pictures of Paris, Hong Kong and Venice and opened the doors of an antique icebox to discover a stereo system and bar hidden inside.

This room opened up into a dining room. It, too, had a

large window, this one, however, held a window seat covered cushions of red velvet trimmed with white lace. Six curve-backed wooden chairs with cushions matching the ones on the window seat flanked a claw-foot oak table. Over the table hung an elaborate three-tiered chandelier, strings of sparkling oval-shaped crystals looped down from one brass candlestick to another, then across to the next one.

"Tanner?" Jill swung into the dining room on her crutches. "What's tucked under your arm?"

"Clothes. I thought maybe, well, actually, I hoped, this was a more modern cabin than mine and had a bathtub. It's been quite a while since I've had a good soak in one and the creek is a little too cold for bathing this time of year."

"Sure. I'll fix us something to eat while you're in the tub. The bathroom is right around here." Jill led the way around the open spiral staircase separating the living room, dining room and kitchen. Smooth polished cedar banisters ran parallel to each other as they circled up the center of the house; the steps were carpeted with a deep sculptured pile of black and gray. The bathroom was next to the kitchen. When Jill pushed open the door, Tanner's eyes popped open wide.

"Wow! This house is quite a showplace. I'm not sure I should even set foot in here, let alone take a bath in it." The so-called tub was a raised whirlpool bath of black, gray and white swirled marble, edged in gold bars that looked like they should be in a U.S. Mint, a pattern that repeated around the whole room. Above the gold bars were white marble tiles with an occasional spray of red and pink roses painted on them. The room even smelled of roses.

"Yes, it's quite a showplace alright. There are towels in the cabinet and probably anything else you might need." Tanner noticed a strange tone in Jill's voice. She walked out, closing the door behind her, a little harder than might have been necessary.

Tanner wondered briefly at the bitterness in Jill's voice, but a clean body called. He filled the tub, stripped off his clothes and lowered himself into the warm, soothing water. He laid his head back on the ledge and relaxed as strains of Johnny Mathias singing "Chances Are" seeped in through the door.

The sound of a whisk meeting the sides of a glass bowl filtered in too, reminding him of the woman in the next room as he dozed off.

Jill knocked on the door and called to Tanner, "You alive in there?"

"Yup. Just laying here relaxing." His old nature would have asked her to join him. Thankfully, this time he thought before speaking. Taming the old beasts could be difficult at times, but God always got him through it. He thought of the verse that had become his mantra. *I can do all things through Christ who strengthens me.*

"If you don't get out pretty soon you're going to look like a prune and the omelets will be too cold to eat."

"Okay, if you insist." Tanner figured Jill must have moved on since the only sounds he now heard were the rattle of plates and silverware. He quickly rose from the water, dried off and dressed.

Jill stood at the stove waiting to flip an omelet and thinking about the work she had gone through to clean years of dust and grime off an old 1915 Sterling wood stove so it could be converted to electricity and used it in her kitchen. It was in storage now, along with a lot of old furniture pieces she spent a lot of time stripping and refinishing. The house she shared with Tom had been his before their marriage, he hadn't bothered to change the title over to both their names and he was so far behind in payments the bank had repossessed it when Jill couldn't come up with the money.

The stove Jill was using was also a converted old Sterling. She and her father had more in common than she realized. Except that infidelity would *never* be added to her side of the list.

The sound of the door clicking shut made Jill turn. She sucked in her breath at sight of the blonde adonis coming toward her. He was wearing a royal blue flannel shirt reflecting the brilliant sapphire of eyes that no longer looked like cold steel, but rather like warm pools of inviting temptation. Damp curls of gold clung to his forehead. He came and stood next to her, looking into her eyes and sending her heart racing.

How she could have thought this man to be cold and cruel just proved you couldn't trust first impressions. He was a warm and fun-loving kind of man, whose gentle, quiet ways were working their way into Jill's heart. She suddenly realized it wasn't just passion she felt for this man, but something much deeper. She remembered reading somewhere you couldn't search for a soul mate, but once he crossed your path you would recognize him and it would be like a thunderbolt hit you. Well, a thunderbolt had hit her in the form of one David Patrick Tanner. Now the question was—what was she going to do about it? Use the feminine wiles she'd heard so much about? She wasn't even sure she knew what they were, much less how to use them, but there had to be some way to convince this man he wanted and needed her as much as she did him.

As Tanner's warm, soft lips met hers, Jill let go of all the doubts plaguing her and replaced them with hope. The hope her kiss would tell him what she wasn't able to put into words, at least not yet.

CHAPTER 14

The long kiss ended, leaving Jill feeling breathless. Fighting for control over her emotions, she turned her attention to the omelet that was getting too done. Her hand shook as she placed it on a plate and handed it to Tanner.

He slid into the corner of the L-shaped booth and picked up his fork, but instead of digging into the tempting confection he laid it back down and asked, "Do you mind if I pray before we eat?"

"No, of course not," Jill was so surprised she was sure she was stammering.

Tanner reached over and placed his hand over Jill's. "Lord, we thank you for this wonderful food you have provided. Please heal Jill's leg quickly and give her a safe trip home."

Tears suddenly felt as if they were forming in Jill's eyes. She fought them, not wanting Tanner to see. No one had ever prayed out loud for her. It felt strange, but at the same time very comforting.

Tanner observed the kitchen as he ate a plate-sized omelet

filled with large chunks of ham, cheese, onion, and green pepper, washing it down with a steaming cup of coffee. Cabinets of highly polished red cedar lined the room; a clock ticked loudly as its pendulum swung back and forth; cast iron pans hung on the wall near the old cook stove. This room was filled with antiques, as were the others he had seen. Some of them, like the stove and the icebox, had been converted into usefulness, others were for show only.

Jill's nearness left him feeling unsettled.

"So you found someone to come and get you in the morning?"

"Yes. Carrie and Jack will be here about 10 o'clock"

Carrie he had heard about, but who was Jack? A small flicker of jealousy passed though Tanner at the mention of another man's name, and he had to admit feeling more than he wanted to for this woman. Should he question Jill about the man or leave it until he met him and could decide what their relationship was then? He decided to wait.

Jill was uncomfortable wearing the same large pants and sweater from Maybelle she had worn for days. She needed to get some clean clothes from upstairs but hadn't been able to figure out how she was going to maneuver the steps to get there. She hated having to ask, but there seemed no other way. "Tanner, could I ask a favor of you?"

"Depends on what it is," he said with a teasing grin.

"Would you go up to the south bedroom and get me some fresh clothes so I can clean up, too?"

"Sure." Tanner slid out of the booth and stood facing her. "What do you want me to get?"

"In the suitcase is a pink jogging outfit. It should fit over this cast. And…and…the other stuff is in there, too." Jill's face flushed bright red. She had never asked a man to get underclothes for her before and, even with Tom, she had always been somewhat shy. But Tanner didn't scoff at her embarrassment; instead he smiled at her with understanding and bounded up the steps.

Tanner reached the top of the spiraling steps and headed for the room at the south end of the hallway. Its door was open, giving a clear view of a white iron bed with a coverlet of bright yellow flowers with green leaves set on a background of white. A white wicker dressing table and cushioned chair upholstered in the same pattern as the bed cover filled the opposite corner of the room, a chest of drawers stood near a window curtained with the same yellow-flowered fabric. The room was bright and cheerful.

Tanner flipped open the suitcase laying on top of the bed and found the jogging suit, socks and underwear all packed in neatly separated piles. He gathered the clothing and carried it back down to Jill.

"Thank you. I'll clean up these dishes, then go change."

"I've got a better idea. You go freshen up and I'll do the dishes."

Jill nodded and went into the bathroom. She stood quietly for a while listening to the sound of water running into the kitchen sink. She looked at the whirlpool and yearned to get in it, instead she took a sponge bath, brushed her unruly hair, applied a minimal amount of makeup and dabbed on a touch of her favorite perfume—Obsession. A grin reflected from her face as she looked into the mirror and comprehended the humor in wearing a perfume whose name meant the domination of one's thoughts or feelings. Which was exactly what she wanted. She wanted Tanner to become obsessed with her. She knew it was crazy, but she still wanted it.

Jill entered the living room and stopped, leaning on the

crutches as she took in the romantic picture of Tanner as he lay on the bearskin rug in front of the flickering fire. His head was propped up by the bear's and his lean muscular body stretched out beyond the length of the rug.

Jill stood frozen for a moment, hypnotized by the dancing fire, imagining her dad and Melissa on that same bearskin. She always thought their family was perfect, until the day a policeman showed up at her door. He explained about her father dying of a heart attack at a cabin in the mountains she knew nothing about. But that wasn't the worst of it. He also told her about the woman who was with her dad when he died—Melissa Fletcher—his other wife. It had been impossible for Jill to believe her father was a bigamist, but eventually the whole truth came out.

Tanner saw an awful sadness envelope Jill's face. He rose from the floor and took Jill into his arms. He kissed her softly, then pressed his cheek next to hers and just held her close, until he felt the moisture of tears trickling down Jill's face. Alarm rose up in him. Had he hurt her? How could he have been so thoughtless as to not remember her broken leg? He was so wrapped up in the tenderness of a kiss he had forgotten. He looked into tear-fill eyes. "I'm sorry, Jill. I didn't mean to hurt you."

Her voice squeaked out, "You didn't."

Tanner's blue eyes drew dark with concern. "Why are you crying then?"

Jill could see that Tanner would accept nothing short of an explanation, but how do you explain the betrayal of the two most important men in your life—your husband and your father. "I... it's...you didn't hurt me or do anything wrong. Now, please, can we forget it?"

"Yes, but are you sure you don't want to talk about it?"

"There's nothing to talk about."

Suspicion weaved its way into Tanner's thoughts as he watched the firelight glow on Jill's alabaster skin. Something was definitely wrong, women don't cry for no reason. Could it have something to do with memories of her husband, or maybe this man, Jack, who was coming to get her? He could see he would get no answers so he scooped her up in his arms and carried her up the stairs, careful not to bang her cast on the banisters. "You need to rest. You've been on that leg long enough."

"I don't think this is such a good idea, Tanner. I can lay on the sofa downstairs"

"It's okay. Trust me."

Jill laughed. "Trust you? The last time you said that you got me drunk on moonshine." Besides it wasn't Tanner that Jill didn't trust, it was herself.

As Tanner approached the room with Jill's suitcase, Jill's face turned pale. "No, not this bedroom, Tanner. I can't sleep here. Take me back downstairs."

"Care to explain what the problem is?"

"No. If you won't take me downstairs at least put me in the other bedroom." Jill didn't want to explain that right before she went outside for her fateful skiing trip, she had discovered this bedroom must have been the one used by her father and his…What would she call that woman if she were to try to tell Tanner about her father's other *so-called* wife? Maybe she shouldn't be mad at Melissa, but surely the woman must have suspected something. Granted her mother had no clue of what was happening, but then she had lived many years as the wife of a traveling salesman.

"But I thought, since your suitcase was in here…"

"Please, Tanner, I don't want to argue about this."

"Okay, whatever you say." Tanner swung around and moved quickly to the other bedroom. The décor was on the opposite end of the spectrum as the room they just left. Calming sea blue and pale green enveloped them as Tanner deposited Jill on the bed and exited the room with a simple, "Rest well."

CHAPTER 15

She couldn't believe she had slept not only the afternoon away, but also the night. Morning greeted Jill with a cheerful hello by sending the bright sunlight streaming through the unshaded windows. Self-reproach overwhelmed her conscience for letting herself want a man she hardly knew and the risk she took by accepting his kisses. A small amount of guilt nagged at her for the way Tom was forgotten while she was in Tanner's arms, until she remembered the other woman who was with her husband when he died.

Jill stared at the tiny flecks of dust floating in the sunbeam arching into the room and landing on the floor, spreading its light like a circular rug of gold on the polished hardwood floor. She wondered what would happen now. Would she ever again see the long golden waves of hair flowing from beneath Tanner's coonskin cap? Would she ever see the face of the man hidden behind the full beard, or learn about the man hidden inside—his past, his present, his hopes, his dreams?

She wanted to feel his lips on hers, and his arms around her once more. But fear of what she might see, or not see, in his eyes kept her from it. She was a proud woman, one who would not ask to see him again, but rather, would wait for him to say he wanted to see her. In this day and age, women told men what they wanted, but that had never been her style, it probably never would be.

~~~~~~~~

Tanner was standing in the doorway watching Jill stare into space and wondering what kind of thoughts were going through her mind. Her hair was tousled, her cheeks glowed a healthy blush pink color, her lips curved downward in a sad expression.

"Good morning, Jill."

"Good morning." Jill felt Tanner looking at her but was afraid to return his look. "Are you hungry?"

"Yes." A slow smile spread over Tanner's face.

Jill started to get out of bed, but Tanner's hand restrained her, igniting the feelings she felt the night before. Feelings that must be ignored. There were too many complications to let this go any further. "I'll go fix some breakfast if you let me up."

Tanner kept his arm across her body. "And how do you propose to do that? It seems you have forgotten about those steep, winding steps that would be difficult and dangerous for you to navigate." His eyes searched hers. "Looks like you're my prisoner up here until I decide to take you down."

The teasing smile Jill had become so familiar with in the last few days, once again crossed Tanner's face.

She forced a scowling look at Tanner and half-heartedly attempted to break free of his grip, struggling with the laughter threatening to erupt from her.
~~~~~~~~

His arms tightened around her and just as he leaned in to kiss her once more, Jill pushed him away.

"I think we'd better get downstairs. Carrie and Jack will be here soon." Jill waited for Tanner to say something, anything, about her leaving but no words came. No declarations he couldn't live without her, no promises of seeing her again. It was probably just as well, but Jill felt as if she'd been set adrift in a sea of loneliness. The words "alone again, naturally" popped into her head. Why did she keep losing the ones she loved? First, Tom. Theirs hadn't been a marriage without problems, but it had made her feel secure, at least until the end. Carrie and her boyfriend, Jack, were her lifeline after Tom's death. She owed them a lot, and soon they would come to her rescue once again. They would take her away from a man with whom Jill could have no more than what had already been, a wonderful interlude. One she could never forget, one it would break her heart to remember.

Tanner sat on the edge of the bed. Time was passing and neither of them talked about what happened between them. He didn't want her to leave, but he couldn't ask her to stay. The phone ringing quickly propelled him back down to the kitchen.

When he returned to the bedroom, Jill was standing by the window watching light snowflakes as they descended to the already covered ground. Everything she wore matched in color, from purple socks and jogging pants that almost hid the cast, to the pale lavender of a sweater that looked as if it were inviting you to touch its bunny-fur softness. She was a classy-looking lady even in baggy pants and loose sweaters.

"Who called?" Jill asked.

"Someone named Melissa. She said to tell you she would try to reach you when you get home. Are you ready?"

Jill didn't comment, just turned away from the window

and studied Tanner. She drank in the way his blonde hair fell in waves to his shoulders and deep blue eyes set into a face covered with a bushy beard of golden curls. It was going to be harder to leave than she imagined. "Yes, I guess I am. If you want to carry the suitcase, I'll try to hobble down the stairs."

"I don't think so, Miss Independence. The last thing you need is to fall and re-injure that leg." Tanner lifted her into his arms once more, thinking of all the times he held her body close to his. More than likely, it was the last time he ever would. She was going home, and her leaving felt worse than anything he had ever known. He finally had to admit to himself he was in love with the tiny, gorgeous creature his arms were wrapped around. It was something he hadn't planned, something that could go nowhere given the circumstances and responsibilities of their lives.

The sound of a snowplow on the road running past the house and a glance at the digital clock on the dresser told Jill her friends would arrive in a matter of thirty minutes or less. She certainly didn't want them to find her in the arms of this mountain man. "Well, carry me down quickly then, please. I have things to do before Carrie and Jack get here." *Like make sure you are out of here before they come,* she thought, but didn't say.

Jill made certain everything was in its proper place and the fire was completely out while she waited for Tanner to carry down her suitcase. She fluffed up the fur on the bearskin rug, thought about how romantic it would have been to lie there on the floor by the fire, and forced the thoughts from her mind by recalling the impossibility of a long term relationship with Tanner. He had his mountains; she had her child and a business to run in the city.

Tanner set the suitcase by the door and walked to Jill. He

turned her to face him. With his hands on her shoulders, he looked deep into eyes that made him think of smooth, melted chocolate. He wanted to tell her how much he cared for her, instead he said sternly, "I want you to go to a doctor and have that leg checked out as soon as you get home. Promise me you will."

"Yes, okay, I will." Jill didn't want the tears forming in her eyes to spill in front of Tanner. "Thank you for all you did for me. You don't have to wait. I'll be fine by myself until they get here."

Tanner watched Jill's eyes turn glassy and a tiny drop of moisture ease out and cling to her long dark eyelashes. He wanted to wipe away the tears, take her in his arms, and tell her he loved her and somehow they would find a way to be together, but he knew it would be building false hopes for both of them. A clean break would be best. He dropped his hands from her shoulders at the sound of a car coming up the lane. His hand gently swept down the side of her delicately freckled face. "Take care of yourself," were the only words he was able to say before the door burst open and a tall beautiful blonde swept into the room and embraced Jill.

A man with features perfect enough to be a model followed her and slipped Jill into his embrace. "Thank God, you're all right. We've been worried sick," he said as he held Jill away from him as if to check and make sure she had all the necessary body parts.

The blonde ran an appraising look over Tanner with eyes the color of summer grass and requested, "Who's your friend, Jill?"

Jill was caught. The well-learned and practiced manners of many years required her to introduce her friends to Tanner, even though she dreaded all the questions sure to follow. She had told Carrie only that she had injured her leg and needed someone to drive her car home. Now explanations would have to be given. "This is David Tanner. Tanner, this is Carrie and her boyfriend, Jack."

"Glad to meet you," Jack removed one arm from Carrie's shoulder and offered his hand to Tanner while he kept his other arm wrapped around Jill, "and thanks for taking care of our friend."

"It was my pleasure." Tanner smiled as he looked directly at Jill and noticed the blush creeping across her face. He noticed, too, the way Carrie was watching them exchange looks of hidden meaning and he decided it was time for him to leave. "I'd better get going. Take care of yourself, Jill, and remember your promise."

"I will," Jill choked out as she watched Tanner put on his buckskin coat and walk out of the door, and out of her life, without a backward glance.

CHAPTER 16

Jack drove Jill's car while she rode with Carrie and tried to evade the questions Carrie persisted in asking.

"You're sure being closed mouthed about that man, Jill."

"You mean Tanner?" Jill was hesitant about answering some of Carrie's questions and some she knew she couldn't answer because, quite simply, she didn't know the answers. "There's really not much to tell. He found me, he put my leg in this cast and he brought me back to the cabin."

Carrie had been able to tell there was much more between Jill and Tanner by the way they looked at each other, but since Jill wasn't ready to talk about it there was no point in trying to coax information out of her.

As they neared the city limits of Knoxville, Jill turned in her seat and looked back at the snow-covered mountains in the distant background. She realized she had come to a deeper understanding of who she was during her stay up there. Things that seemed important before no longer were. Her time on the mountain had touched her with a simpler, quieter way of life and she wondered if she would be able to handle the hectic pace of life in the city again. She thought of Tanner and could almost understand his need to be alone in the wilderness, but that didn't stop the hurt she felt at his leaving without a word about wanting to see her again. She knew it wasn't practical to think they could continue a relationship, but she still wanted to hear him say it.

When Carrie pulled into the driveway of the ranch-style house they shared, a dark haired little boy ran to greet them. Jill acknowledged she was home, her time on the mountain was over and it was time to go on with her life.

~~~~~~~~

Tanner decided to go check on Maybelle and the baby before he went home. W.H. was sitting at the table with Ned when Tanner entered the cabin. He looked up and said, "Boy, ya look as if the whole durn world jest blew up in yer face. What's ailin' ya?"

"Nothing. I'm fine. I just came to check on Maybelle and the little one."

"I'll git her." Ned said as he rose and entered the bedroom at the back of the cabin.

"Here. Looks like you could use a swig o' this." W.H. handed Tanner a jug of moonshine. " Maybelle done tol' me about thet gal ya took home with ya. She got anythin' ta do with ya havin' the dismals today?"

"No." Tanner hadn't meant to be so brusque with the old man, but what he was feeling really wasn't anybody's business but his own. He pushed the jug away. Since becoming a Christian, alcoholic drinks no longer held any interest for him.

"Sounds like a real ripper ta me. Ain't no point in lyin' ta
~~~~~~~~

yerself, boy, or ta me. I seen enough folks a heart-burnin' in my day. Even had a case o' it once myself. Thought I wasn't fitten for to knock at her door, so I didn't. Let some other fellow come along and steal 'er away. Still think about 'er sometimes." W.H. took a long drink of the moonshine and passed the jug back to Tanner. "Not thet I ain't happy with Ma, it's just, well, I don't think ya ever forget a heart-rending thet makes ya feel like ya been hung up by yer tail and left out ta dry."

For some odd reason, W.H.'s story loosened Tanner's tongue. "That's about how I feel—hung up. I wanted to keep her here with me, but things just wouldn't have worked. She has a small son and a business in Knoxville."

W.H. stroked his thinning beard. "Um, I see. A city gal. Sounds like ya got real trouble there. I was jest a pup when yer gran'daddy brought one up ta the mountain. She didn't' like it up here, said the livin' was too hard and took off like a haint was after her. I don't think he ever did hear from her agin."

"No, I'm sure he didn't. My father told me the story. Said grandpa refused to change a thing, expected her to change her lifestyle to the way the mountain women lived and not complain, even though she was used to having things much easier. She finally got fed up and left.

"Yep, city gals is used ta things bein' easier. Sure ain't gonna keep one here living' like ya do. Ain't nothin' changed at thet place o' yer gran'daddy's since he was here. Ya jest moved in and continued ta live as if ya were tryin' ta make him proud o' ya bein' able to live like he did."

"Wasn't any reason to change anything. I've been getting along fine." Tanner felt as if W.H., in his round-about way, was trying to tell him something. He wished for once the old man would just come out with it and not make him try to figure it out for himself. "Just what, exactly, are you trying to tell me?"

W.H. gave Tanner a toothless smile. "Well, boy, it's like this. If ya wanta keep a woman happy, ya gotta step a little higher." Without another word, W.H. left the cabin.

As Maybelle and Ned sat down at the table, Tanner questioned, " Did you hear what he said?"

They both nodded.

"What was he talking about, Ned? I swear sometimes I don't know how you ever grew up knowing anything, the way that man puts things."

Ned laughed. "He makes ya think, doesn't he? That's always been Pa's way. He never told us what he thought we should do. Instead he gave us words o' wisdom ta help us try and figure things out fer ourselves."

"Well, that 'Ya gotta step a little higher' wisdom of his is going to take a lot of thinking for me to figure out what it means."

Tanner checked over the baby and Maybelle and found them doing well. He traveled the same trail he and Jill had taken back to his cabin. Everything reminded him of Jill. Dirty dishes were still scattered on the table and counter since they left in his angry rush. He flopped down on the bed, her soft musky smell still lingered. The quiet never bothered him before but now he had difficulty falling asleep, he kept waiting to hear the sound of Jill's soft breathing.

Weeks went by. He hunted, he worked on his experiments with the plants, and he paced the rough hewn boards of the cabin floor. He tried to get Jill off his mind, but it didn't work. He could still hear her gentle voice. He could almost feel her soft kiss as he wrapped his arms around a pillow and tried to sleep each night. W.H.'s words rang in his head until, at last, he came to an understanding of what the old man meant, and made a decision not to let this woman get away. He felt really happy for the first time in his life. He began to formulate a plan.

~~~~~~~~

Life sucked Jill up into its raging river once again. Between the hectic pace of keeping her thriving business going and trying to spend time with Alex, she was once again on a merry-go-round with little time for herself. But even with the fast pace of her life, Tanner was on her mind almost constantly, the worst times being when she was alone in bed at night remembering—the sound of his laughter, his kisses. Sleep didn't come easily and it was beginning to show in the tiny tired-looking lines forming around her eyes.

Carrie tried to get her to talk about Tanner, but what was there to tell? She'd grown to care about a man she knew nothing about. It was over. She had to put it away, along with all the other things of the past that hadn't worked out the way she wanted them. She tried dating, but no one made her feel what she felt with Tanner. He could make her heart race just by looking into her eyes.

A month had passed since she'd seen Tanner. Now, it was almost Christmas. The stores were brightly decorated and their windows displayed all the perfect gifts to give your loved ones. Carrie's two sons and Alex grew more excited as each day passed, bringing them closer to the day when they would receive all their wished-for presents. Jill and Carrie purchased a huge tree, which totally filled one corner of their large living room. They decorated it with an eclectic mixture of new and old ornaments. The bubble lights that had been on Jill's Christmas tree every year since she was a child fascinated the boys as
~~~~~~~~

they watched the bubbles bounce their way to the top of the brightly-colored, translucent glass.

But Jill was neither excited by the glitter nor waiting in expectancy for Christmas to come this year. She felt alone, sad.

One night after putting Alex to bed, Jill sat staring at the blinking lights of the Christmas tree and wondering where Tanner would spend Christmas. The doorbell chimed and Jill heard Carrie's voice saying, "Yes? What can I do for you?"

Jill heard the deep masculine voice request, "I'd like to see Jill." She sat stark still listening to Tanner's voice, wondering if her desire to see him again had tricked her into believing he was actually there.

Carrie entered the living room with a tall, well-built man who Jill would not have recognized if it hadn't been for his hypnotic blue eyes. "Look who's here, Jill." Carrie smiled at the two of them lost in each other's eyes and discreetly left the room.

Jill stammered, "You look…so…different." She scrutinized the new Tanner. His curly golden beard was gone; only a neatly trimmed mustache remained, giving him a much younger, even boyish, look. A faint scar running from the corner of his eye to the cleft of his chin was a reminder of the mountain lion's attack. Gone was the long flowing wavy hair. Instead, the collar-length style barely touched the top of his ears as it was brushed back on the sides. A few unruly curls still fell on his forehead as if they were saying, "You can't make us change." He wore a black shirt, black dress pants, and black shoes which shone with the gloss of a high polish. His camel-colored jacket was accented by a perfectly knotted tie with a maze—like pattern of camel and black. He looked nothing like the man Jill had met and fallen in love with on the mountain.

Tanner put his hands around her face. His lips lowered to

hers, tenderly tasting their sweetness. "You look exactly the same as I have pictured you every night and every day since you've been gone."

Jill felt her body go limp, her legs begin to feel weak and trembly. Tanner's arms went around her as his lips returned to hers. She could feel one heart beating, pounding. She was unsure if it was Tanner's or hers.

The slight break of his lips leaving hers brought Jill to her senses. She knew nothing about this man. She needed answers before she would let herself be charmed by him this time.

Jill pressed her hands on his chest and pushed Tanner away. She took a deep breath. "We can't let this go any further, Tanner. At least, not until you answer a few questions.

CHAPTER 17

"Okay." Tanner said with a smile. "What do you want to know?" He had come to Jill with the intention of telling her everything, so this time he didn't feel threatened by her questions.

"For starters I want to know why a doctor is hiding out in the mountains, and who are the people in the pictures in your trunk?"

Tanner walked over to the window and looked out at lightly falling snow as the street light shone on it. "Well, where do I start? The woman in the picture is my wife, Emily." He turned in time to see Jill's face turn red with anger and hurriedly went on to explain. "That is, she was my wife until she died three years ago. A year before her death, my brother died after being in a boating accident. Everything just got to me, so a few months after Em's death I went to live in the mountains."

When Jill didn't say anything, he continued, "I just couldn't handle being around people. When they laughed and joked about things, I wanted to shout at them, 'How can you be so happy? Don't you know how I'm hurting.' But of course, they didn't know, they couldn't understand because they had never tried to survive the loss of someone they loved. I think they had it right when people were allowed to have a whole year of mourning. Anyway, it was just too difficult, so I left."

"You ran away?" Jill didn't like the sound of Tanner not facing life. She had wanted to get away from her problems after Tom died, but leaving just wasn't something she could do.

"It wasn't really running away. I needed time to accept all that happened and figure out what to do with the rest of my life. I was tired of living my life the way everyone else wanted me to long before Emily and Tim died, but it wasn't until Tim died I realized life is too short to be so unhappy all the time. So I began to search for some meaning for my life and that's when I found God."

"What do you mean, you found God?" Jill questioned. She had the inane desire to say she didn't know He was lost, but thought better of it since Tanner's look was so serious.

"It's hard to explain. I had gone to church all my life, but never really had a relationship with God. I believed in Him, that He created the world and all, but I wasn't sure of much else. I tried every church in Knoxville. Finally I came to a small church where the pastor said there is a verse in the Bible that says if you diligently seek God, you will find Him.

After hearing his sermon, I felt a burning need to have some quiet time in order to get to know God, to develop a relationship with him, and to find out who Jesus and the Holy Spirit were. I heard about them in church for years, but never really understood how to have them in my life. My time in the mountains has given me the solitude to develop that relationship." Tanner wanted to share more of what he learned with Jill but he could see she wasn't ready yet.

Jill listened quietly while Tanner talked. All this God talk was making her a little nervous. Was he some kind of fanatic? She wanted to know what his intentions were, but was afraid to ask. Besides, she wasn't sure she wanted to get involved. Could she trust him? She thought she could trust Tom, but found out she was wrong.

Tanner pulled Jill into his arms and held her. "We belong together, Jill. You know it and I know it. How about we get things settled here and you come home to the mountains with me."

Immediately red flags went up for Jill. Once again, someone else was making decisions about her life. What if she didn't want Tanner, which of course she did, but he hadn't bothered to ask what she wanted, he only told her the way it was going to be. And what about her business, and Alex, and could she live in a one room shack with no electricity or running water? And even though he claimed to be a Christian, he hadn't said a word about marriage, only that she should come to the mountain with him.

"I think you're moving a little too fast here, Tanner." Jill moved out of his arms and went to sit on the sofa.

Tanner joined her and took her hands in his. "I know. I'm sorry. We have a lot to talk about and I shouldn't have been so pushy. It's just that ever since you left the mountain, you were all I could think about. You even got in the way of my research."

"Research?"

"Yes. Did you know that worldwide one of every ten plants is used for food, and one in six is used as medicine?" Before Jill could answer, Tanner continued, "There are over 275,000 species of plants ranging from tiny algae, that can live below the surface of the snow, to a sequoia, weighing as much as 2,500 tons. A large part of the world's population still relies on plants and their crude extracts as their only affordable source of medicine. For example, cloves have been used medicinally for thousands of years in Southeast Asia. The unopened buds of the clove tree are sun-dried and used for treating infections, including malaria, cholera and tuberculosis. They are even used for digestive problems like gas, colic and abdominal bloating, as well as a stimulant to strengthen contractions during childbirth.

"Native people of Guatemala use the pulp of avocados to stimulate hair growth, the rind to expel worms and the seeds to treat diarrhea. In Africa, the aloe vera plant has a long history as an effective healer of wounds and burns. Cleopatra was said to attribute her legendary beauty to aloe vera."

Tanner took a breath and continued, "Herbal medicines have traditionally been effective remedies for a variety of human ailments. There are projects going on in other countries right now teaching women how to use herbs for healing. Due to shortages of conventional medicine in poor countries this seems like a logical solution."

Jill was fascinated. "So tell me how your research is going to help."

"Well, my goal is to consolidate the knowledge of the mountaineers and other herbalists into a small book. Through a mission project called Seeds for Life, we would send seeds or started plants to countries with little or no health care available. The book would be printed in each of their languages and have directions for growing, harvesting, and using the herbs."

She was impressed and felt a little foolish at the thoughts she remembered having about him being a killer hiding out in the mountains, but then he need never know that.

Tanner stood and stretched, then reached out to Jill to join him. "Well, it's getting late and I've had a long day. Since tomorrow is Sunday and you don't have to work, I thought maybe I could come get you and your son. We could go to church and spend the day together. Church services are 10 o'clock. So, do you want to go?"

At the word *church,* Jill's heart clutched. Panic welled up, closing her throat. She swallowed several times, attempting to answer Tanner. The last time she had been in a church was Tom's funeral. Was she still mad at Tom? Mad at God? Or was it the memory of Tom's death and the days that followed she couldn't face? Maybe it was time to move on with her life. If she was going to have a relationship with Tanner it would include going to church, so she might as well agree to go with him.

"Yes, Tanner."

"Great. I'll see you in the morning." He handed Jill a business card reading *TANNER MEDICAL CLINICS, SAMUEL L. TANNER, M.D.*; a business number and a home number were listed on opposite bottom corners. "My father's," he explained. "I'm staying at their house while I'm here."

"How long are you planning on staying?"

"Don't know yet. Depends on how long it takes to convince this beautiful lady I know she can't live without me." Tanner smiled at Jill, kissed her good-night and left.

Jill headed down the hall to her bedroom, but noticed Carrie's door partly open and the light on. She pushed the door open. Carrie looked up from the book she was reading and asked, "So, what's up?"

"I need to talk about Tanner. You got the time?"

"Sure." Carrie patted the bed beside her and Jill sat down. They talked long into the night. When Jill finally left the room, she still wasn't sure what she wanted to do. She hoped morning would bring answers.

But morning didn't bring answers, instead it brought more questions. When Tanner didn't show up to get her and Alex for church, Jill tried to call the number he had given her, but there was no answer. She tried repeatedly, until at noon she finally gave up. Fuming, she grabbed her coat and Alex's and announced to Carrie that they were going for a walk and to tell Tanner, if and when he called, he'd better have a darn good excuse for not showing up and not being around when she called.

When she and Alex returned from their walk, Carrie gave her a message that Dr. and Mrs. Tanner's housekeeper called stating there had been a family emergency and David would call her as soon as he could.

~~~~~~~~

Tanner scrubbed and put on the required garments for surgery. He hadn't operated since he had watched his wife die on an operating table. He wasn't performing this operation, either, but Connie insisted she wouldn't have it done unless he was present. His thoughts ran back to earlier this morning. He'd been having a cup of coffee with his mother when Connie walked in. She'd been a part of his family since they were kids, so knocking wasn't expected. They had grown up living next door to each other. Their parents had done everything and gone everywhere together, a friendship that lasted until both of Connie's parents died. Now his parents were in the waiting room, praying, as he was, that Connie would survive the heart surgery.

Guilt plagued Tanner. He caused the attack. He hadn't thought about the heart condition she'd had since childhood. The complex heart defect, called tetralogy of Fallot, had been repaired with open heart surgery soon after her birth due to a severely narrowed pulmonary artery. The defect required
~~~~~~~~

lifelong medical care from a specialist. Now something had gone wrong and surgery was necessary to save Connie's life.

He could have been easier on her when he told her he was going to marry Jill, but when she started yelling, "This is the thanks I get for waiting all these years? Now you're marrying another woman? I can change, David. Just give me another chance. I know you want a Christian wife, so I will become one. Is Jill a Christian?"

"Well, not exactly, but…"

"Don't marry her! I can be the wife you need. I'll go to church, we can adopt a child, whatever you want, just tell me."

Tanner thought about the time he considered marrying Connie. He could have accepted the fact that they would never be able to have children of their own, but Connie refused to even discuss adopting. It was a constant source of argument between them. He thought about Jill's little boy who he was to have met today and hoped Mattie had been able to reach Jill to explain why he wasn't there when she called.

A nurse Tanner didn't recognize stepped into the room. "They're ready to start, Dr. Tanner."

Six hours later the surgery was finished, but Connie's life still hung by a thread. Tanner stayed by her side and, as she came out of the anesthesia, reassured her that he would stay with her. He slept on a cot moved into her private room, barely able to leave for a cup of coffee without her getting upset over his absence.

He called Jill, explaining only that a family member had a heart attack and he needed to stay at the hospital. Tanner didn't want to tell Jill over the phone about Connie, it would be better if he explained in person.

His parents insisted that she couldn't be alone when she went home in a few days. A maid wasn't enough; she needed a doctor close by "just in case". They wanted him to stay with her, but Tanner came up with a compromise. Connie could move into his parent's house until she was well enough to go home. There she would have not only two doctors at her beck and call, but his mother to pamper her and their maid to wait on her.

While they were getting Connie ready to go home from the hospital, Tanner slipped out of the room to call Jill. She wasn't in the shop; her assistant said she was at a client's house. He left a message that he would call again later, but when he arrived home with Connie, Mattie met him with a message that Jill called. After getting Connie settled in an upstairs bedroom, he went downstairs to return her call.

She answered on the second ring, "Hi. I thought maybe you went back up the mountain until I got your message. How is your family member doing?"

Jill's bright, cheerfulness was just what he needed. Tanner smiled. Just the sound of her voice made him feel like he could handle all the problems in the world. "Fine, now that I've heard your sweet voice. I can't get away today, but how about meeting me tomorrow for lunch at The Bistro?"

Jill hesitated. They hadn't seen each other in over a week and now she had to tell him she couldn't meet him for lunch. "I'm sorry, but I can't tomorrow." She heard Tanner groan, but went on. "I have to go out of town for a few days. I'll be returning on Wednesday. Why don't I call you when I get back?"

"Don't you think it would be better to stay in town and off that leg? It won't heal properly if you don't take care of it."

"So says the doctor," Jill laughed. "I can't stop doing my job or I won't have a business. The time I took off has caused some financial problems already."

"Okay, but remember to be careful. Call me as soon as you

get back. I've really missed you, Jill. I love you, darlin' and I'll see you on Wednesday." Tanner hung up the phone, but not before he heard the click of an extension hanging up before him.

CHAPTER 18

Tanner said he loved her. He'd said it for the first time over the telephone. Jill didn't know whether to laugh or to cry. But tears spilled down her face as she thought about how much it meant to hear those three little words.

She sailed through getting books, sketches and samples ready to show her new clients, then went home to pack enough clothes for two days. She wished she was able to see Tanner before she left, but he at least had given her something to hold on to until they were together again. Only two short days and she would be able to feel his arms around her again.

By the time she got on the plane early Wednesday morning to return home, Jill was frustrated and ready to leave Virginia. What her clients wanted was next to impossible. They had built an elaborate log house in the Alleghenies and wanted it furnished with items that looked antique but were usable. Not only that, but they wanted most of the furnishings hand-made, like quilts, pottery, and even most of the furniture. They wanted to feel as if they were stepping back in time. All the modern conveniences were to be hidden from sight so a visitor wouldn't even know they were there.

The worst part of it was, they wanted it done in three months. They were willing to pay the price, but first Jill had to be able to find all they wanted. Her briefcase was loaded with pictures and drawings of designs they created themselves. This job was going to be a royal pain, but if she could pull it off it would mean financial freedom, as well as put her on the top of the list of most sought after interior decorators east of the Mississippi.

Carrie picked her up at the airport and whisked her home. She played with Alex for a short time, called Tanner to set up a time for them to meet, then she went to her shop. She was excited about the new job, but didn't have time to think about it because she had to hurry to an appointment with a client before meeting Tanner at the restaurant.

She saw him the minute she entered. He sat at a table facing the door . He smiled and waved a hand at her. Her heart pounded as he gave her a brief hug before she sat down. It seemed like such a long time since she had seen him. She drank in his good looks, his smooth deep voice and his heart-capturing smile. She sensed he was creating conversation in order to avoid talking about something and was suddenly afraid his feelings for her changed in the two short days she was gone.

"Okay, Tanner, what is it? What's bothering you?"

Tanner looked up from the coffee cup he had been staring into. He should have been surprised she could read him so well, but he wasn't. It was nice to know the person you love could sense your feelings, but frightening at the same time. He had been dreading this moment. "I need to tell you about Connie."

"Connie?" Years of practice at hiding her emotions surfaced. Her voice remained level, sounding cold and unconcerned even to her own ears. Her throat felt as if someone was wrapping a rope around it and steadily tightening it. Flight seemed the appropriate action, but her body refused to move.

Tanner knew he had to tell Jill everything, even though he may lose her. The thought made him feel empty and alone. More alone than he felt when the snow held him captive for weeks on the mountain. But she had to know, she had to trust him. He hoped once she heard the whole story she would understand.

Connie caused him trouble when he was married to Emily, so he figured it could happen again. Jill needed to be prepared.

"Connie and I have a unique relationship. We grew up living next door, we're the same age and our parents were best friends. Her parents died in a plane crash when we were seniors in high school so she came to live with us until graduation. She went to the same college as me, she even applied for medical school but was turned down because of her heart condition. We spent a lot of time together and Connie assumed we would get married. I guess I even thought that for a while. Connie was comfortable, and since I grew up in a don't-rock-the-boat type of family, I went along with the plans she started to make for our wedding. I hadn't gotten around to getting her an engagement ring. It seemed like every time I started into a jewelry shop I froze up and couldn't go through with it. Then I met Emily."

Jill watched emotion pass over Tanners face; love and sadness fought for space. He took a deep breath.

"Go on," Jill encouraged.

"Emily was on the opposite side of the spectrum from Connie. Connie was an ordered life, a plan for everything; she lived as if perfection were an obtainable goal. Emily was fun, frivolity, wild clothes and living life at high speed." Tanner ran his hand down his cheeks and chin, missing the soft beard that had covered his face for the better part of three years. "Once I met Emily, marrying Connie was out of the question. I realized

I didn't love her the way a husband should, what I felt was more brotherly, so I called off the wedding. Em and I married three months later."

Why is it, all the men in my life aren't able to stick with one woman? I said I would never again get involved with a man, but I did, and now look where it got me. Jill fumed; she bit her lip.

Jill's face was unreadable. Tanner waited a few minutes. "Aren't you going to say anything?"

"What is there to say? You did what you thought was best."

"I did, but Connie never really got over it. She didn't marry, stayed in her parent's house next door to Mom and Dad all these years. "

There was more to the story, Jill could feel it. Something Tanner wasn't telling her. She waited quietly, watching Tanner repeatedly pull his watch away from his wrist and letting it snap back; any pain it might have caused not being felt. When she could stand the wait no longer, she prompted, "And?"

"She's never accepted that I don't love her. She still insists we belong together, that I will marry her someday." The next words out of Tanner's mouth came out in a rush, as if saying them fast would make them easier to say. "I may be spending some time with her for a while. She just got out of the hospital. She had a heart attack. The doctors say she'll be fine, but needs a lot of rest and can't get excited or upset."

"Is she the one you spent all that time with at the hospital?"

Tanner nodded his head. "Yes."

"Why didn't you tell me right away when it happened?"

"I wanted to tell you in person, not try and explain it over the phone."

"Where is she now?" Jill knew the answer even before Tanner spoke the words.

"At my parents." Tanner watched Jill's eyes flash with anger, her small supple body grow rigid, her otherwise soft-pink complexion flush red hot.

"But that's where you're staying, isn't it?" Both hands tightened on Jill's coffee cup. She wished she could throw something. She was losing control. Now wouldn't that be different, the always cool, calm, collected Jill out of control. But then ever since she met Tanner, her emotions swung from the highest peak to the lowest valley. Her palms were damp, her heart raced, but her mind focused only on one fact. Tanner was staying because of another woman.

"Yes, but it means nothing, Jill. I've…"

"It means nothing? How can you say that? You are living in the same house with a woman who wants to be your wife." Why was it that all the men she loved always turned to another woman? What was wrong with her that she wasn't enough for them?

Tanner tried to remain calm. It wouldn't do any good to have both of them angry and screaming at each other. "I thought I left all that behind when I went to the mountains. I didn't want to marry Connie. I didn't want to be in a medical practice with my father. I didn't want to try and explain again and again to everyone why or how my outlook on life changed so much. They just didn't get it. I thought my parents would after having lost one son, but I guess they thought my leaving was like losing their only remaining child. They accused me of running away instead of facing my problems.

"But I wasn't running away; I was running to. To having time to explore my new faith in God. Time without people trying to get me to do what they wanted, but rather to find out what God wanted me to do with the rest of my life. I was pretty sure Connie was not a part of that plan."

Tanner's two large hands reached for and captured her small left hand. His fingers rotated a ruby ring that replaced the wedding rings that were still on her finger the last time he had seen her. He was glad she had taken them off at last. His eyes searched hers for some sign of acquiescence. "I don't want her. I want you."

"Then prove it." Jill pulled her hand away. Knowing she was being unreasonable didn't stop her from blundering on like a bulldozer in search of a building to destroy. "Move out." Uncertainty gripped her. She learned long ago that men did not like ultimatums, that they usually chose the opposite of what you wanted just to prove they would not relinquish control to you, but that didn't stop her.

"I can't do that. She's sick, I'm a doctor. It's as simple as that."

Blind jealousy made her press the issue. "Your father is also a doctor, is he not? He can take care of her."

"Yes, he could, but she insists I stay, and right now she's not supposed to be put under any kind of stress. Look, Jill, there's no reason this should affect us. We can still see each other. It's only a matter of time until she's well enough for me to leave."

The waitress appeared at their table, momentarily stalling the conversation as she refilled their cups with hot, steaming coffee, giving Jill a chance to think about what Tanner just said.

In less than a week of being snowbound with a stranger in the mountains, she had found the kind of love she never would have thought possible. And now, for the second time in her life, another woman was involved, and she couldn't go through the pain of wondering what was happening between them.

"Jill?" *What is she thinking?* Tanner wondered as he watched her stare into the amber-colored glass lantern in the center of the table. Its flame danced a fast rhythm, equaling the pounding of his heart. He couldn't lose this woman, he must do something to convince her he loved and wanted only her. Yet instinct told him it was better not to push her. She seemed to be an intelligent woman, one who wouldn't let emotion get in the way of rational thinking. He was sure she would accept the situation,

Her mother's voice echoed in Jill's head as she remembered words spoken as they left the office of her father's lawyer, "I'll never, ever have anything to do with another man. They are nothing but trouble."

Jill was beginning to agree with her mother. Disappointment reigned, first with her husband, Tom, then her father, now Tanner.

"I can't, Tanner. I can't go on seeing you while you and Connie are living in the same house." Her eyes met his. She watched them turn from entreatingly soft to the cold blue steel she remembered from the first time she encountered them.

"You *can't?"* Anger filled him. "For heaven's sake, all I'm asking for is a little patience and to keep seeing you."

Jill grabbed her purse from the chair next to her, flung the strap over her shoulder and grabbed her crutches. "Make your choice, her or me," she said as she turned too quickly, a crutch falling. Tanner reached out to help steady her, but she slapped his hand away, bent over and picked up the crutch, then stomped away, very ungracefully. Bells jingled as she pulled open the door and held it open with a crutch until she could hop through.

Carefully avoiding the sidewalk's few icy spots with her crutches, she made her way around the corner and down one block to her shop. She didn't notice the woman in dark sunglasses following her, or see her stop to read the sign on the door stating the name and business hours of her shop after Jill had gone inside. Neither did Jill see her go into The Bistro and walk up to the table where Tanner sat dejectedly twirling an empty coffee cup in his hands.

"Hello, David."

"Connie. What are you doing here"?

"May I join you?"

"Sure, but you shouldn't even be going out yet. Why aren't you at home resting?"

"That's all I have been doing, and you said yourself I needed to start getting up and around."

"I know, but I didn't mean coming downtown yet."

Connie surveyed the interior of The Bistro at the Bijou as the waitress brought her coffee and refilled Tanner's cup. "Remember when we used to come here for dinner, then go to the ballet at the Bijou Theatre? I never did understand why they didn't change the name of it when they restored it."

Tanner looked at the fashionably dressed woman sitting across from him. "A lot of things don't change, Connie." *Like the way you are trying to manipulate me again by bringing up the things we enjoyed in the past, only this time I'm not going to fall for it,* Tanner thought. Immediate freedom from Connie was what he wanted, but he would have to wait until her condition was stable.

"Let's eat dinner here together. I know it's early but that way we'll miss the theatre crowd."

"I don't' think…"

"Come on, David, just for old time's sake. Or were you meeting someone else?"

"No, I'm not." Tanner planned on taking Jill out to dinner, but that hadn't worked out and he needed to eat somewhere since he told Mattie he wouldn't be home. He made a quick decision, hoping he wouldn't regret it, and asked the waitress for two menus.

~~~~~~~~
~~~~~~~~

Jill slammed the new catalogs that just arrived on her desk and tried to sit down and concentrate on them, but all she could think about was Tanner. The anger and betrayal she felt began to leave her, and regret that she acted so hastily and so childishly took its place. Maybe if she hurried, Tanner would still be there. She grabbed her coat, put in on while standing on one foot and once again attempted to hurry while moving on crutches, an almost impossible task.

When she re-entered The Bistro she saw Tanner still sitting at the same table—with another woman. He hadn't seen Jill yet, he was busy concentrating on the menu. She quickly slipped back outside. *Well, he certainly didn't wait long to find someone else.*

~~~~~~~~~

Melissa took a deep breath trying to get ready for what she knew was going to be a difficult task when she saw Jill come out of her shop, go down a few doors and enter The Bistro. Within minutes, Jill exited the café and was returning to her shop. Melissa almost laughed out loud at the sight of Jill slamming her crutches on the sidewalk with every step she took.

Once again the time wasn't right to approach Jill about her—*problem.*
~~~~~~~~~

CHAPTER 19

The next morning Jill sat at her desk staring at pictures of the log house she was to have done in a short time, but was unable to concentrate on them. Instead she kept seeing Tanner and another woman, just as she had in restless dreams all night. When Tanner called last night, she told Carrie to tell him she didn't want to talk. It was childish, but she didn't care. The last thing she needed right now was to be caught in the middle of a love triangle.

Someone was pounding loudly on the shop door. Jill came in early, but hadn't yet opened for business. She glanced at the clock hanging on the wall and wondered who would be trying to get in this early. The store didn't open for another hour. She decided maybe her assistant, Anna, also planned to start early today, but forgot her key, as she had a bad habit of doing. It was one of those little things that bothered Jill, but otherwise Anna did such a good job, Jill couldn't fault her for this one bad habit.

She came out of her office and stopped still on her crutches.

Through the glass door, she could see Tanner standing on the other side. His broad shoulders were hunched, as if that would keep the cold wind from getting through the turned up collar of his coat. His forehead was creased with scowl lines and Jill read his lips as they coaxed her to let him inside.

Her hands gripped the smooth wooden bars of her crutches tightly as she swung past the cash register counter and to the front door to release the dead bolt and let in the last person in the world she wanted to see this morning. She wasn't a morning person in the first place and to make matters worse, she had yet to have her first cup of coffee. She felt grouchy and out of sorts. Between the lack of sleep Tanner caused her and the impending argument she knew was coming, she felt like she would enjoy scratching out his beguiling blue eyes as soon as he walked through the door.

Tanner heard the deadbolt click, but waited for Jill to back up on her crutches before pushing on the door. A gust of wind proceeded Tanner in through the open door, sending the hem of Jill's long, full circle skirt skittering up to reveal a cast with signatures sprawled across it. Her head was bent down, and the expression on her face reminded Tanner of a bull snorting and pawing, preparing to charge.

"We need to talk." Tanner looked into shadowed eyes that told him there was more to the problem than he thought.

Jill turned slightly away from Tanner, trying to shrug off the hand gently touching her shoulder. "There's nothing to talk about."

"Yes, there is, and I don't think the whole problem is Connie. What else is bothering you, Jill?" He wrapped his arms around her and held her close. Then pressed his cheek against the top of her ebony hair, hoping that if he didn't look at her directly, she would be able to open up and tell him what she was feeling.

Jill felt the thin veneer of protection she had placed over her emotions begin to crack. Somehow Tanner had the ability to make her feel it was safe to talk about how she felt, that he wouldn't laugh at her or tell her she shouldn't feel the way she did. Seeing him with another woman brought back the anguish Tom's death caused.

Jill thought she and Tom had a good marriage. She wasn't prepared for the possibility of him being unfaithful to her. She tried to reassure herself that there was some logical explanation for another woman being with Tom when his car slid on treacherous ice and careened over the mountainside and into a ravine, killing both Tom and his female passenger instantly. Friends and family all told her Tom wasn't that kind of man, that he loved Jill. But doubts had niggled at her mind for the past year and since Tom was dead, she would never know the truth. She faced that fact eventually and convinced herself that the woman must have been a hitchhiker or something like that. Now the doubts were raised, again. Tears slipped from her tightly closed eyes while she fought for control over the sobs threatening to jerk her enclosed body.

Tanner noticed the passers-by gawking in at them through the plate glass window at the front of the shop. "Is there someplace private we can go?"

Jill pointed a curved finger toward the partially open door that held a sign announcing it to be an office. Her crutches banged to the floor as Tanner lifted her into his arms. "My crutches."

"You don't need them," Tanner said as he carried her into the office and, with her still in his arms, sat down on a mauve rose-patterned sofa. His feet pushed carefully at the coffee table stacked high with catalogs, swatches of material, and samples of floor coverings in order to give himself more leg room. With calloused fingers he wiped the moisture from Jill's cheeks and tenderly touched her lips with his.

"Jill? Jill, are you all ri...," Anna's voice trailed off as she entered the office and viewed the surprised looks and flushed faces of her boss and a ruggedly handsome man. "I'm so sorry. I didn't know...I mean, well, I thought something happened to you when I saw your crutches lying on the floor of the showroom."

With as much dignity as she could muster, Jill thanked Anna for her concern as the woman backed out of the office with a large go-for-it grin and closed the door behind her.

Jill rocked with laughter as Anna left the room. "Did you see the look on her face? It made me feel like a teenager who got caught necking on the front porch swing."

"Yeah, me too. What do you say to taking the day off and spending it with me?"

"I don't know, Tanner. I've got an awful lot of work to do."

"Can't you at least take the morning?"

His arms wrapped tightly around her as if he knew he must hold on or she would move away. He hated to tell her that this was the only time they would have to spend together for a while. "I'm going back to the mountain tomorrow, Jill."

The words were spoken so softly Jill wasn't sure she heard him right. "You're what?"

Tanner looked at hair the color of a raven's wing spilling over Jill's shoulders in soft curls and sought eyes so dark they almost matched the color of her hair. "I said I have to go back to the mountain tomorrow. I'd like us to spend some time together before I leave so we can iron out a few things."

Jill's heart fell. Tanner was leaving. He probably wanted to tell her it was over between them. But the memory of his passionate kisses of only moments ago assured her that couldn't be what he wanted to talk to her about. Throwing caution to the wind, she agreed to spend part of the day with him. She hopped on one foot over to the phone on her desk, dialed her home number and informed the sitter that she would be out of the office for a while. After Tanner retrieved her crutches, Jill went into the showroom and announced to Anna that she was leaving, maybe even for the whole day.

She giggled as she eased her way into the soft leather seat of the red Porsche Tanner parked directly in front of her shop and said, “I feel like a kid skipping school.”

Tanner moved the seat back so her cast leg could be stretched out in front of her, closed the door, and moved around the car to the driver’s side. He glanced up as he opened it and noticed a sleek gold Cadillac parked at the end of the block on the opposite side of the street. His body tensed immediately. What was Connie doing spying on him? Had she followed him from Wilson’s Bed and Breakfast this morning? He purposely had avoided the hotel he usually stayed in when he came home for a visit. So how had she found him?

Last night their dinner was pleasant, even friendly. It first appeared that Connie had changed, for once she wanted nothing from Tanner, but he had been wrong. When she brought up the subject of a marriage between them and when Tanner said no, she exploded, and once again, the real Connie showed her true colors.

Emily’s death, Connie’s demands and his father’s persistence had all been factors in his flight to the solitude of a remote wilderness. In the last three years Tanner discovered the trappings of the rich life were no longer for him. He found that belief in God was the only thing able to bring the kind of peace in one’s life that truly mattered.

Like Ma Tuttle once said, “ Yer ne’er gonna see a wagon

filled with my belonging's bein' toted ta my buryin' ground, so it don't matter what I have here anyways, cuz the Good Lord'll take care o' me jest fine when I git up yonder."

He slid behind the wheel of his mother's car and chuckled at the thought of his mode of transportation over the three years he spent on the mountain.. He answered Jill's questioning look, "I was just comparing Jake to this car. I think I like Jake better." He glanced into the Cadillac that had no occupant as they drove past it and concluded that there must be hundreds of cars just like it. He was foolish to think Connie was following him. It would serve no purpose. The relationship she wanted never really started, but it was definitely over. He told her so last night.

Jill watched the sun glint off the glass window panes of tall skyscrapers and smoke puff from chimney stacks of factories as they whizzed past. *Tanner will be gone tomorrow* echoed in her head as she tried to make light conversation with the man whose hand held hers. The tanned skin of his large hands made hers look white and small. She felt an aching desperation to hear him say he couldn't leave her, but she knew that wouldn't happen. This day could be the last she would see him and she intended to enjoy every second of it.

Jill scowled as Tanner slowed to enter the driveway of Wilson's Bed & Breakfast. Jill stayed here once with Tom and loved it. It was an 1865 antebellum plantation home that had been restored. There was talk that it was soon to be listed in the National Registry of Historic Places. Each of its eight bedrooms were furnished with antiques, a bathroom en-suite, and a fireplace. She and Tom had enjoyed the Grecian swimming pool, the summer splendor of the gardens and the gazebo. Those memories were best forgotten but how was she to explain to Tanner? Instead she simply asked, "Why are we stopping here?"

"I thought we could have breakfast and talk without anyone interrupting us here." Tanner watched Jill's eyebrows move closer together in a frown. "Is there something wrong?"

"No. I…" Jill searched for the right words. She couldn't very well tell Tanner she spent a night here with Tom. "I was just surprised that you chose this place, that's all."

As they entered the grand vestibule of the fourteen room house, Jill hoped they would be able to avoid the owner who was standing close by talking to another couple, but he spotted them and excused himself. "How nice to see you again, Mrs. Morgan. It's been a long time."

Jill took his extended hand and replied, "Yes, it has. I'm surprised you remembered me."

He looked at Tanner as he patted Jill's hand and smiled broadly, "A beautiful woman is not so easy to forget. You are a blessed man, Mr. Morgan."

Jill watched Tanner in amusement as the owner walked away. His eyes flashed as he mumbled, "Remembers you from a long time ago, but me, who just checked in last night, he forgets. Let's go." Tanner strode to the winding staircase and started up, then stopped suddenly, as if he just remembered something important.

Jill managed the first step with her crutches before Tanner roughly picked her up. She said, "I can do it. Now put me down."

"I'm not putting you down. You'll fall trying to get up those steps with that long skirt. Just hold on to the crutches and be quiet, woman. I didn't think about the dining room being on the second floor when I brought you here."

A revelation of sorts came to Tanner. In his arms was a woman who gave so much to everyone. He wondered why God chose to give him another chance at love.

When he first met Emily, he thought she was the one for him, but the closer they got to the wedding date, the more unsure he became. He should have listened to the little voice inside of him telling him to back out of it. But he hadn't. Back then he didn't know God would speak to you in a kind of quiet, still voice. One you couldn't hear audibly, but yet you hear it. It's something so hard to explain to anyone that Tanner never tried, he just remained in awe of it.

This time he was asking God's opinion. No uneasy feeling came, no silent whisper telling him to stop. Instead he felt at ease, sure the relationship between him and Jill was one God wanted him to pursue.

He would move heaven and earth to keep Jill, and that might be exactly what it would take to remake his home in the mountains into a place where she could be happy. He thought of the plans he had drawn up for remodeling the one room cabin. He would build a wind generator for electricity, which would pump water from the springhouse to the inside of the cabin. There would also be a road for easier access to their home. He hadn't told Jill of his plans, nor would he. It was going to take some time to construct it all and he wanted to wait until he could ask her to marry him before he showed it to her.

Once seated at their table, they looked out at the coating of snow that covered flower gardens waiting for the warmth of spring in order to burst forth in the profusion of color Jill remembered. They talked in depth about their lives, each hoping the other would come to a deeper understanding of what made them who they are today.

Jill gained an insight as to why Tanner was such a quiet man about his hopes and dreams. All his life he had been told they were foolish, unreasonable and impractical. But Jill thought they were wonderful and told him so, for where would this world be without dreamers like Thomas Edison, Henry Ford and the Wright Brothers. She admired him for his determination to help the world become a place where people who did not have access to medical advice could grow their own medicine for some illnesses and be taught how to use it.

Jill told Tanner about the new log house and its eccentric owners, who wanted their own pattern of pottery created, as well as numerous other unusual furnishings, and her doubts about being able to find everything they wanted.

A broad smile lit Tanner's face as Jill's need brought the solution to how he was going to be able to see her before he finished the work on his place. "That shouldn't be any problem for you. The Tuttle's are a clay clan."

"A clay clan? What is that?"

"I mean they are potters. They make all their own dishes, churns, pickling crocks and jugs. They have their own pug mill."

"What's a pug mill?"

"It's a machine in which materials, like clay, are simultaneously ground and mixed with water or some other liquid."

Ideas and possibilities filled Jill's mind, but there was one major problem. "But I don't know how to get to their place."

"That's no problem. I can meet you and take you there. When do you want to go?"

Jill did some quick calculations in her head. "How about a month from now? We can meet at the cabin and you can show me the road to get there.

Tanner threw back his head and laughed. "Jill, there are no roads leading back there, only a trail."

His hand caressed her warm cheek; his eyes fell into the depths of hers. "I love you. I know it's going to be tough, but somehow we'll figure out a way to make it work so we can be together." A surprised look came over Jill's face and he questioned whether he should have said anything yet. "That is, if that's what you want," he amended.

"Yes, I want that, too. I want to be…" Jill let the words she was going to say die. He hadn't actually spelled out what he wanted. Did he mean marriage or seeing each other once every few months, or what? She couldn't ask. She had made the move to spend time with him and even though the matter of his being in the restaurant with Connie was cleared up some doubts still existed. Trust was difficult for Jill. The next move would have to be his. For some reason she couldn't explain, she felt uneasy, as if something or someone was going to stand in the way of their being together.

Tanner reached into his coat pocket and pulled out a small box wrapped in satiny red paper and topped with a tiny white bow. He handed the box to Jill, "Merry Christmas, Love. I couldn't wait until Christmas."

Tears filled Jill's eyes as she read the card that hung by golden threads from the bow. "I give you my heart. Love, Tanner." Slowly, she unwrapped the paper. Inside a box of blue velvet, a golden heart dangled from a chain of gold. Tiny diamonds sparkled from the bouquet of flowers etched on the front of the locket. She drew it out of the box and held it in her fingers as tears slid down her cheeks. "Oh, Tanner. It's beautiful."

"Turn it over."

Engraved on the back was the same message as was on the card. Her heart swelled with love for the man sitting across the table from her. His eyes were filled with the question of whether she liked his gift. At that moment he reminded her of Alex after he drew a picture for Jill and waited anxiously for her approval.

"I love it. It's beautiful and I love you, too." But it wasn't a ring. The question of marriage remained.

CHAPTER 20

The rest of the tables were now void of people. One waiter stood near the drink station looking bored, swinging a towel around, impatiently waiting for them to finish their meal so he could clean off their table.

Regretfully, Tanner slid his chair back, "I guess we'd better go."

"Yes, I suppose we better." Jill got up from the table, painfully aware that their time together was nearing an end. She had a sudden thought, she was sure Tanner wouldn't be driving a Porsche into the mountains. "How are you getting back to the cabin?"

"I have a Jeep I take as far as Chet's Trading Post, park it there and walk the rest of the way. *For now anyway, until I get the trail widened enough for a vehicle to pass through,* Tanner thought.

After Jill put her coat on, her handbag slung over her shoulder and crutches in hand, Tanner held out his arms to her. "Your carriage awaits, madam." He scooped her up, gave her a quick kiss on the end of her nose and reluctantly left the dining room.

Being carried made her feel delicate and very feminine. She wondered if it would ever happen again once the cast was gone. Jill snuggled close in Tanner's arms. The light, fresh, piney scent of his lingering cologne reminded her of his cabin in the woods and she wondered how she could keep her business going and live in the mountains. Tanner had said they would find a way, she had to believe him.

She loved her work, but without someone to share her dreams and success, it wasn't quite as wonderful. She never really liked the retail end of the business. That was Tom's forte' and he had been very good at it. She often told him he could sell snow skis to an African. She wanted to be able to choose the jobs that were a real challenge, like the one she was working on now. She learned long ago that a house told many things about the people who lived in it. You could find out their occupation, meet their family by pictures and tell if they were strait-laced and conforming or adventurous. They say people look like the kind of dog they choose to have for a pet, but to Jill, the way they choose to decorate the interior of their house tells of their heart.

"Now what would you like to do?" Tanner asked.

"Would you like to meet my son, Alex?" Jill needed to know how Alex was going to react to Tanner before she got so involved with him she couldn't walk away. It was probably already too late to turn back now.

Tanner accepted Jill's offer and they were soon speeding down the interstate. He thought how little he knew about Jill.

"Tell me about your family," he said. When she said nothing he glanced over the same tight closed-in expression he had seen before when Jill didn't want to talk about something. Once again he wondered why it was so difficult for Jill to talk about her family.

"Not much to tell," she finally said softy. "I'm an only child. My mom and dad live….no," she swallowed hard before continuing. "I mean, my mom lives here in Knoxville. Dad died five months ago." She stopped speaking. How could she tell Tanner about her father and his…what would she call her? She wasn't his wife, not really. Her father was a bigamist, what an ugly word. Even uglier were the thoughts she was having about the woman who had devastated her mother's belief that she had a good marriage to a wonderful man.

~~~~~~~~~

Melissa's hand shook. She reached her finger out to the doorbell once more and pressed twice. Her right foot tapped repeatedly on the wooden boards of the porch while she waited for someone to answer the door. She couldn't hear any signs of life in the house, but a car sat in the driveway. She had to be here. Melissa had to get this conversation over with. It couldn't wait any longer.

No one came. She pushed the white button again, rapidly, three times. Suddenly, as she stood in the cold tapping her foot, she felt a sturdy kick. The baby kept moving around until he had a foot stuck in her ribs. She smiled as she rubbed her side, gently pushing on the protruding foot trying to force it out of the uncomfortable position. Laughter bubbled up until she was giggling uncontrollably. This whole situation wasn't funny, but she couldn't seem to stop. Tears rolled down her cheeks.

A car door slammed. Melissa looked toward the street and watched a tall muscular man hand crutches to Jill and close the car door. One minute she was concentrating on the getting up
~~~~~~~~~

on the crutches and the next, after looking up to see Melissa on the porch, she was growling, "Get me out of here, Tanner. I don't want to talk to that woman." Jill jerked open the car door, flopped onto the seat, tossed the crutches into the back, and slammed the door so hard the window rattled.

Tanner looked at Jill, then at Melissa. Raising his hands in an "I'm sorry" gesture, he walked back to the driver's door.

"Come back, please, Jill," Melissa called out, moving down the steps so swiftly she didn't notice the spot of ice on the second step until it was too late. Her arms flew out, her body arched backward; her head smacked the top step.

Tanner ran to the woman. Blood was already pooling on the step by the time he reached her. "Call an ambulance, Jill. She's hurt badly," he yelled at the car's closed door. When Jill didn't respond, he ran up the porch steps and into the house to make the call himself.

Jill couldn't move. She stared in shock at the young woman lying on the steps, her large stomach protruding. A baby. Her father's baby. Jill hadn't known. *So, what are you going to do about it?* It had been a long time since she had heard the silent voice of God, but she still recognized it. She tried to argue. *I'm not sure it is Dad's baby.* God responded with silence. She knew she had to make a decision, and quickly. A baby. Dad would have been so happy. He had always enjoyed it when the house was full of Jill's friends. He had spent many hours playing baseball in their back lot with all the neighborhood kids.

Again she heard, S*o, what are you going to do?* She knew she couldn't leave Melissa laying there injured without at least trying to help. Stretching, she reached into the back seat and grabbed the crutches, pushed the car door open and carefully worked her way up the sidewalk to the porch.

She took the scarf from around her neck and, gently lifting

Melissa's head, laid a cushion between it and the hard porch. Blood came away with her hand. Staring at it, she began to pray, "Lord, please help Melissa. Don't let anything happen to her or her baby. And forgive me for being so, so…pigheaded and unfeeling. This whole mess really wasn't her fault, but it is so hard to imagine my father could do such a thing to her and to my mother."

The door banged shut as Jill finished her prayer. Looking up she saw Tanner's smile. Sirens shrieked loudly as the ambulance arrived. Soon two EMTs requested Jill move out of the way. They attached an oxygen mask and a blood pressure cuff, while another EMT, clipboard in hand, asked Jill questions, " Name?"

Jill stuttered, trying to get out the words, but they wouldn't come.

"Do you know this woman?"

"Well, sort of."

"Do you know her name?"

"Yes, it's Melissa…Fletcher."

"Address?"

"I don't know?" Jill felt the EMTs scowl.

"Next of kin?"

"I don't know. Look, just take her to the hospital and get her awake so she can answer all your questions herself."

At his nod, the others swiftly loaded Melissa into the ambulance. The two jumped in the back; the questioner moved into the driver's seat, started the vehicle, and slipped it into gear. Flipping on the siren, he looked at Jill; his eyebrows drawing together toward the middle of his forehead in the biggest scowl Jill had ever seen. Dirt flew up as he stomped on the gas and made a hasty departure. The ambulance wobbled slightly when the driver took the corner a little too fast, then it disappeared out of sight.

Jill leaned on her crutches, staring at the ambulance as it left. How was she going to explain to Tanner who Melissa was? How was she going to tell him her father was an adulterer, a bigamist? That Melissa's baby was most likely her brother or sister.

Just tell the truth. She heard, but she wasn't sure why God was suddenly speaking to her after He had been quiet for so long. What was it Tanner had said? When you didn't hear God, it wasn't because He had moved away, but rather you had.

She felt Tanner's arm slide around her shoulders. "Jill? Are you okay?" Before she could respond, he added, "Who was that woman?"

Looking into eyes filled with confusion, Jill answered, "Let's go to the hospital. I'll explain on the way."

As they made their way to check on Melissa, Jill simply said as fast as she could, "My father was a bigamist. Melissa was his other wife. I knew nothing about it until he died of a heart attack, with her, at the cabin."

"The cabin on Blue Mountain? The one I took you back to? But you said…"

"I know, I wasn't truthful with you, Tanner, because I didn't want to talk about what my father had done. Now that there's a baby involved, it seems like I can't get away from it. Oh…"

"What? Tanner saw that something had suddenly dawned on Jill.

"How am I going to tell Mom about this…this baby? She was so devastated when she found out about Dad and Melissa. Oh, Tanner, what am I going to do about this whole mess?" Jill covered her face with both hands as she sobbed, giving Tanner the impression she felt she needed to hide her tears, her sorrow, from him.

He slid the car into the first empty parking spot he could

find in the hospital's lot. Reaching over, he pulled Jill's hands away from her face. "Let's just take this one step at a time. We'll go see if Melissa has regained consciousness. If she has, you can find out if the baby is your father's. Once you know the answer to that question, you can figure out how to deal with your mother. First, though, before we go in, I think we should pray."

Jill nodded in agreement and Tanner began, "Lord, Your Word says that by Jesus' stripes we are healed. We ask for healing for Melissa and that no harm come to the baby. Also, we ask You to make it clear to Jill how to handle the situation with Melissa and with her mother. Help them to forgive. We thank you, in Jesus' name."

"Amen." Jill added, too deeply touched to say more.

Once inside the hospital, they learned Melissa had regained consciousness soon after arriving at the hospital, then gone into labor. They were directed to the waiting room near the maternity ward.

Several hours later, and after they downed as many cups of sludge masquerading as coffee as they could stand, Jill called Carrie to let her know it may be a while before she would be home and would explain then.

Jill began to have second thoughts about whether she should even be waiting for Melissa to have her baby and was about to tell Tanner she wanted to go home when a nurse dressed in white pants and a top covered with little pink and blue bears entered the room.

"Are you Jill?" she asked.

"Yes." Obviously, Jill thought, since she was the only woman in the room, but didn't say it.

"Mrs. Fletcher would like you to be in the delivery room with her."

"But, I…No, I don't think….Are you sure?" She turned to Tanner. "What do you think? Should I?" But before he could answer, she went on, "Someone in her family should be with her, not me."

The nurse smiled indulgently, as if she already knew the whole sordid story. "She says you are her family and that's good enough for me. Come on," the nurse grabbed Jill's crutches from the floor, handed them to her and helped her stand. "She needs someone to hold her hand while the little one enters this wonderful world."

Jill glanced at Tanner questioningly. "There's nothing like seeing a baby born, Jill," he reassured her.

"But I already have. Remember. I have a son."

The bear-uniformed nurse put in, "Ah, but it's different when you're not experiencing the pain. You can enjoy it more."

Feeling like a chicken ready to go under the ax, Jill followed the nurse into the delivery room. Melissa laid panting, blonde curls plastered to her face by the trickling sweat. When the contraction slowed its intensity, Melissa turned toward Jill. "Thank you for coming."

"Shouldn't your mother or someone from your family be here with you," Jill asked.

Such a sad look passed over Melissa's face it made Jill want to take back the words, though she didn't know why.

"I don't have any other family, Jill. I was abandoned by my mother when I was a baby, then adopted by an older couple when I was four. My father died when I was eight, mother when I was thirteen. Since they had no family who wanted a child that wasn't of their blood, I ended up in a group home until I graduated from high school. Life was horrible," another pain took her, yet she was able to whisper, "until I met Phil."

Compassion engulfed Jill. How would it feel to be so alone?

She couldn't even imagine. The nurse handed Jill a cool-damp cloth, motioning for her to use it. While gently wiping the sweat from Melissa's face, Jill remembered the breathing techniques Tom had helped her with when she was in labor with Alex. Suddenly she found herself coaching Melissa and smiling at the thought of soon meeting her new brother, or sister.

~~~~~~~~

Another man entered the waiting room, hindering the pacing Tanner had been doing across the rather small room. It had been three hours since he and Jill had entered the hospital, one since she had left him for the delivery room. He had been told nothing since then.

"Did you faint, too? Is that why you're in here?" the man asked.

"No, I'm not the father."

"Oh." The man sat on one of the hard plastic chairs lining half of the room. Why he hadn't taken the more comfortable sofa, was a question soon answered. "I don't deserve her," he mumbled to the floor as he sat slumped over. "She's the one going through all the pain and I fainted. Fainted, not because of any blood, mind you, just because.... Oh, I don't' know why I fainted, I just did. How am I going to explain this to her? She'll never forgive me."

Just as Tanner was about to console the man, Jill entered the room. A look of unbelievable wonder topped a beaming smile. "I have a sister, Tanner. You should see her. She has Dad's black curly hair and her eyes are blue, but so dark I think they will be brown like his, too. And guess what Melissa named her? Samantha Jill. Isn't that something? Do you want to see her?
~~~~~~~~

Come on," Jill grabbed his hand and pulled him out of the room as she explained Melissa's family tree.

Tanner's thoughts went to the Bible verse, "and a child will lead them." This child may be the healing link between Jill and Melissa, and maybe even Jill's mom. The more Tanner saw how God worked, the more he marveled. On his best day, he could never have come up with a plan to take an orphaned woman, a disillusioned daughter and an angry widow and forge an unbreakable bond between them with a newborn child.

~~~~~~~~

Tanner took Jill home and had no more than entered the door than he was bombarded by three noisy little boys. It was easy to see which of them belonged to Jill. Alex had dark hair and eyes, dimples in his cheeks, and was a little quieter than the other two boys. But Alex was soon on his lap as the threesome listened to Tanner's tale of fighting off the ferocious mountain lion.

"Oh, come on now," Carrie chimed in as she carried in a cup of steaming coffee and joined them. "There aren't any mountain lions left up there. I go to my dad's cabin every summer for a month and I've never seen one, nor heard of anyone else seeing one."

Jill reaffirmed Tanner's story. "He's telling the truth, Carrie. I saw it with my own eyes. I just didn't want to tell you about it because I was afraid it might keep you from going up there next summer."

Tanner observed Jill's friend and house-mate; he liked her. The models he had known always seemed to be stuck on themselves and very careful not to let anyone see them without their "face" on. But Carrie's shimmering gold hair was pulled
~~~~~~~~

back in a ponytail and her makeup-free face revealed sculptured features of perfection. Hers was a kind of cool, remote beauty, where Jill's was warm and inviting.

"Guess I better get going." Tanner slid Jill's son from his lap and stood.

"Will you come back and tell us more stories?" questioned Alex.

"Sure I will, and maybe someday your mommy will bring you to see me. Would you like that?"

"Yeah!"

Jill watched as the big man crouched on the floor and talked to Alex. Then he stood and she walked him to the door.

"I'm sorry I can't stay, but Ida Mae's baby is due any day now. It's her first, so I'll go stay at the Tuttle's until the little one is born."

"Who is Ida Mae?"

"She's Ned's sister, who also lives in one of the cabins in the clearing. If I can, I'll come back in two weeks for Christmas, but I can't promise. If there's too much snow on the roads up there for you to be able to travel them when you come next month, I'll give you a call. Otherwise, I'll plan on seeing you." Tanner gave her a long, lingering kiss and left.

Carrie changed clothes and went to work. The babysitter came and took the boys to the mall to see all the Christmas decorations, leaving Jill alone. She puttered around the kitchen. She didn't feel like going back into the shop yet, she was still on a high from all the talking she and Tanner had done.

The doorbell rang. Jill opened the door to find Connie standing on the other side of it. Before Jill could say a word, Connie pushed her way in and started rampaging. "I know you've been with my fiancé'. I've been following you. I saw you kiss him. If you continue to see him I'll nail you to the wall. I'll file charges against you for alienation of affection. I'll see to it that no one ever again darkens the door of your quaint little shop, and I'll make sure your son is taken away from you for being an unfit mother. David will never leave me, no matter what he told you. He loves me and the only reason he is messing around with you is so he can have a child. But I can get him a child. David's father has a lot of power in this town and he wants his son to come back, so I'm sure he'll help me. This is your only warning. Stay away from David." Connie slammed out the door before Jill could utter a word.

Dark thoughts clouded her mind. Was Connie telling the truth? No, it couldn't be. Tanner wasn't the kind of man to tell two women he loved them.

Finally, after much thought her mind was made up. She wasn't going to wait until next month to go up into the mountains; she was going as soon as the cast came off. The sooner she could talk to Tanner, the better. Now that she had a plan, she tackled making the arrangements with a vengeance.

She called the doctor's office and made an appointment for the next day. All she needed to do now was find Chet's Trading Post. Tanner said there was a phone there and it was within walking distance of his cabin. She called information to get the number, dialed it and got Chet on the phone. He gave her explicit directions on how to get there and promised not to tell Tanner and ruin Jill's surprise if he saw him again before she got there.

The more she thought about what Connie said to her, the more upset she got. She was tired of sitting back and suffering the consequences of someone else's actions. It was time she took charge of her life.

CHAPTER 21

How simple Jill's life had been before she broke her leg. Things she never thought about being able to do—like driving a car, walking up steps, taking a bath—were a major chore. She wore long skirts and baggy pants to try and hide the ugly cast. She rubbed her hand over it and thought about when Tanner put it on.

At the time she hadn't know he was a doctor. She thought killer, thief and many other things, but never doctor. After she returned home and the x-rays showed it was set properly, her doctor offered to replace the make-shift cast with a more modern one, but she refused. It gave her a feeling of still having a part of Tanner with her. She missed him; he hadn't made it back for Christmas because of a snowstorm in the mountains.

The doctor wouldn't take Jill's cast off early, which meant she had two more weeks to stew and fret over her relationship with Tanner. During that time, Jill decided to settle the issue of the woman who was with Tom when he died.

~~~~~~~~~

"What do you mean you can't give me that information? Has this got something to do with that privacy law, HIPAA or whatever it's called?" Jill stared hard at the officer who didn't look old enough to be out of high school much less having graduated from the Police Academy. She hoped a little intimidation would get through his defenses.

"No, I didn't mean it like that, Ma'am." He replied. "It's all a matter of public record and not protected by HIPAA, unless there is a criminal case pending, and there isn't. I meant you'll have to go to the courthouse to get that information."

"I'm sorry," Jill said, forcing herself to calm down. "I just need to know who this woman was. She died in a car accident with my husband and it's been eating away at me for over a year. I need some answers." Now embarrassed she had shared so much personal information, Jill quickly thanked the officer and left.

At the courthouse, a woman with huge, dangling, ladybug earrings jotted down Tom's name and the date of the accident. "Do you know if any charges were filed?" she asked. Each time she moved her head one of the red and black bugs slapped her jaw.

Distracted by the sight, Jill answered, "Charges? Uh, no. There was only my husband's car involved, no others. It was raining heavily and for some unknown reason, they skidded and went off the road. The crash killed my husband and his… passenger."

"This should be enough information." With a long red-polished fingernail, the clerk pointed to a wooden bench on the wall opposite the counter, "Have a seat and I'll be back shortly."
~~~~~~~~~

Jill's foot jiggled up and down as she watched people step to the window and make their requests of other clerks. It seemed to be taking forever. She was almost ready to bolt, when the bug lady returned.

"Here we are," she waved some papers at Jill, then slapped them down on the counter and began to read. "Says here there was a 17-year-old girl from New York City with your husband at the time of the crash." She looked up from the paper she was reading, "You gonna write this down, so you don't have to come back and ask again?"

Jill scrounged around for some paper in her purse, finally using the back of a credit card receipt. *What was Tom doing with a 17 year old from New York City?*

Bug Lady continued, "Her name was Sarah Bloomberg, daughter of Ira and Gladys Bloomberg, also of New York City." She flipped to the next page of the report. "Her parents had filed a missing persons report on her just a couple of days before the accident. Police figured from what information they gathered that she was hitchhiking. Her guitar was found in the wreckage so her parents assumed she was trying to get to Memphis in hopes of getting the music she wrote sung by some famous country singer. Poor thing. Anything else I can do for you?"

"No, thank you." Jill left the courthouse. After all this time, she finally had an answer. One she could have had long before this if she hadn't been so stubborn, so afraid of what she would find out. She had been wrong. Tom was not having an affair. He had just picked up a hitchhiker. Having Tom's fidelity settled was a great relief. Now if only she could turn back the clock to before her father cheated on her mother.

Her mother. It was time Jill told her about Melissa's baby, her new little sister. She didn't know what she was going to say, but it had to be done. She and Alex had gone to her mother's early enough on Christmas Day to go to church before having dinner and opening presents. It was a new church for her mother, a little strange to Jill because of all the hugging and arm raising and shouting "Amen", but Mom had seemed much calmer and happier, never once mentioning "that woman". Jill hadn't told her that she and Alex had spent Christmas Eve with "that woman" and her baby. She hoped future holidays weren't going to be like this one—separate, due to the actions of her father.

During the drive to her mother's, Jill tried to figure out how to tell her mother about the baby—her dad's baby. She still didn't have the words when she opened the back door of the home where she had spent her growing-up years. Music filled the kitchen, as her mother's voice blended with a man's singing, "Worthy is the Lamb, worthy is the Lamb. You are holy."

Jill moved in to the living room where she saw her mother, eyes closed, arms stretched upward, swaying and singing. A bright-green-labeled CD spun in a player near where Jill stood mesmerized. Her mother had always attended church, but Jill had never witnessed her doing anything like this before. Her mother, Amanda, had always been pretty, but at this moment she was beautiful, radiant even. Jill hated to interrupt, but she had to get this over with. She pushed the stop button on the CD player. Amanda's eyes opened slowly, a dreamy look in them. She smiled at Jill, but Jill wasn't certain the smile was for her. It seemed as if her mother were in another world.

"Mom?"

"Hi, Jill. I didn't expect to see you today. Did I forget you were coming?"

Her mother seemed back to her normal self now. "No, I…I have something I need to tell you and wanted us to be alone when I did."

"Oh, that doesn't sound good. Want some tea first?"

"Sure, that sounds good." Jill thought maybe it would be better to ease into the subject of Melissa. "What's with the new music? I don't think I've ever heard it before."

"No. It's new to me, too. But, oh, is it powerful. Couldn't you feel it when you came in??

"Feel what?"

"The presence of the Lord," Amanda got a faraway look again as she filled the tea kettle from the tap, set it on the stove and ignited the burner. She pulled out a chair and sat next to Jill at the table. Patting Jill's hand, she asked, "Now what did you want to tell me?"

"First, I want to know more about what's happening with you. You seem…different."

"I am different, Jill. I've been born again."

"Born again? What does that mean? How can you be born again?"

"Jesus said, 'Unless one is born again, he cannot see the kingdom of God.' Oh, Jill, it's so awesome what has happened to me. I was going to tell you, but I needed a little time to digest it all myself. I was water baptized last Sunday, dunked completely under water, and when I came up out of the water, I felt like a brand new person. All my sins were washed away, I was born again. It's so hard to explain the feeling, but it feels like joy is just bubbling up out of me. I want you to feel this; I want everyone to feel this."

"But you've always gone to church Mom, why didn't this happen sooner? Why didn't it happen to me all the years I went?"

Amanda touched Jill's cheek as she said, "I don't know the answer to that, honey. Maybe we just weren't ready to give our hearts completely to Jesus. Maybe the things we've suffered have made us yearn for a strength we don't have on our own."

"Funny, that's almost the same thing Tanner said about being able to forgive others. That we can't do it on our own, but we can with God's strength."

Amanda got up and poured their tea. "You know, I wasn't too happy at first when you told me about Tanner, but if he thinks like that maybe I was wrong. I have been praying the Holy Spirit would show you the way, not only in your relationship to Tanner, but also with God. Now, what did you come here to tell me?"

Jill hesitated; she even issued a small prayer. *Lord, please give me the words. I don't want to hurt her anymore than she already has been.* She took her mother's hand in hers and held it tightly. "Mom, Melissa had a baby a couple of weeks ago. Dad's baby."

Amanda got up and went to the sink. Her back was to Jill. Her shoulders began shaking. Jill got up and went to put her arms around her mother, when she suddenly realized Amanda was laughing, not crying. Worried her mother was having a breakdown, she asked, "What gives, Mom? Why are you laughing about this?"

"Because I think God has been trying to tell me about this. I've been dreaming of a baby every night for weeks. I assumed it was because you were serious about Tanner and that meant I may have more grandchildren. Leave it to God to forewarn me so I wouldn't be so shocked." She smiled at Jill, "I couldn't tell in the dream. Is it a boy or girl?"

"A girl. You're not furious? Or hurt even more by this?"

Amanda shook her head. "I guess I should be, but I'm not. And I have forgiven them. Everything wasn't all your dad's fault, you know. He wanted attention. I didn't give it to him. I was so wrapped up in my job, trying to find good foster homes for all those kids, I didn't even notice his loneliness. Even though he had very little time at home between sales trips, I was too busy to be here when he was home."

Jill was quiet for a while. "I didn't spend much time with him, either. He'd call and I would be busy with Tom and Alex or running the decorating business. Too busy to take time off for my own father. That's sad."

"Okay, that's enough of this sad talk. Your dad is gone and there is nothing we can do about it except ask God's forgiveness for our part in his infidelity. What's her name?"

"Who?"

"The baby, silly."

"Samantha Jill."

"Have you seen her?"

Jill explained the whole story of Samantha's birth to her mother and when she was finished, much to her surprise, Amanda asked her to check and see if Melissa would let her see the baby. She really shouldn't have been surprised, her mother loved children, especially babies. Jill pictured future Christmas celebrations where everyone she loved would be together—just one big happy family.

~~~~~~~~

Finally, Jill was on her way to Tanner's cabin. Carrie had some time off work and was going to keep Alex while she was gone. She pressed down on the accelerator of her Jeep, thankful the vehicle she had just purchased had enough gumption to fly up the steep curving mountain roads. She decided to conquer two problems at once. She could see Tanner and settle the matter of an engagement between Tanner and Connie. Then she would find Tuttle's and get started collecting the things she needed for her client's house. She even formulated a plan to sell her
~~~~~~~~

shop and do interior decorating freelance style. If she could buy homemade quilts, furniture and pottery from the Tuttles, she could specialize in the kind of houses that were decorated with antiques and homemade items. She wouldn't need to do very many of those jobs to make a good living and she would have more time at home with Alex. Somewhere in the back of her mind, her plan had included the possibility that Tanner did want to marry her.

Jill looked out at the pine trees that seemed to surround and hide the road curving off ahead. A shadow passed over the hood of her car. She lifted her foot off the accelerator in order to slow down so she could see what made it. A noble-looking golden eagle rode the wind above Jill, then soared off past the clouds, making her wish she could climb on his back and fly off with him.

Soon she came to a wooden sign that announced Chet's Trading Post was just one mile ahead. The chain-suspended sign flapped and banged in the wind between the two wooden posts holding it. Jill drove past and entered a dirt road barely wider than the Jeep. Soon a log building that looked like it was built by early settlers came into view. Melting snow dripped from the wood-shingled roof into barrels posted at each corner of the store. On top of each barrel was a piece of screen held down by two bricks. A tin sign, with some of its red letters unreadable due to chipped paint, was nailed above the door announcing the place to be "Chet' T ading Pos ".

Jill got out of the Jeep and stretched. The weather was unbelievable for it being January. She pulled open the door, grimacing as it squeaked loudly, and entered, stopping to let her eyes adjust to the dimness. An old man was sleeping in a wooden rocking chair in front of a woodburning stove. A hand-rolled cigarette hung from his lips and a young red-haired pup lay draped across his lap. It opened one of its eyes as she neared, but the dog made no move to get up. Loud snores came from a huge nose that seemed to cover the majority of the man's face and one of his ears was missing. *I'll bet that's an interesting story,* Jill thought.

She looked around to see if anyone else was in the store. It was like taking a step back in time. Furs of various animals were piled high in one corner, sacks of flour, salt, and sugar were lined up on a shelf behind the counter. A pickle barrel gave off a strong vinegar odor, and on the counter the choice of King Edward or Casa Bianca cigars fought for space with paper-wrapped pieces of taffy.

"Kin I he'p ya?"

Jill had been so wrapped up in her observations she hadn't heard the man get up from the chair. "Yes. I'm Jill Morgan. Are you Chet?"

"Yep. Yer made it, huh? Well, I seed Davey yestaday, but I ne'er told 'im ya was a'comin'. Right nice weather fer this time o' year. Ne'er seed one like it. First it snows more'n it's suppose ta, then it gits like spring's a comin'."

Chet gave Jill directions to Tanner's cabin. It was a much longer walk than she expected and she had to stop and rest several times. She watched both sides of the trail, her heart thumping as she thought of the mountain lion that had attacked Tanner and the numerous other wild animals who roamed the woods. She jumped at every sound.

Long before she reached the clearing which held Tanner's cabin, she heard the sounds of a hammer meeting wood. Now she could see him. Her heart skipped a beat as she watched the movements of his muscular body. His head raised, just like an animal when it senses danger. She moved back into the trees and mentally patted herself on the back for wearing a green coat and pants that blended with the tall pines behind her, but it was too late, he had seen her and was moving at a fast pace toward her.

"Jill? What are you doing here?" Tanner lifted her off her feet and twirled her around. Before she could get in a word, he kissed her and put her down. "You're a sight for sore eyes. I was coming into the city tomorrow to surprise you, and now you're here. Couldn't stand to be away from me, huh? How's your leg, Love?"

A large, boyishly-charming grin covered his face. He looked so happy to see her. She hated to wreck his mood, but she was going to have to talk to him about Connie. "My leg is fine, but I think I overdid it with that long walk from Chet's."

Tanner's smile was gone, something was wrong. Jill seemed distant and she was two weeks early. "Why don't you come inside and we can talk about why you're here."

As they neared the front porch of the cabin, Jill paid closer attention to the strange looking thing Tanner was working on when she first saw him. It looked like the propeller of an airplane mounted on the frame of a windmill. "What's that?"

"Just a little experiment I'm working on. I'll tell you about it later. Come on." Tanner took her hand and led her into the cabin.

Jill caught a glimpse of charts and drawings scattered across the table before Tanner picked them up and moved them to the bookshelf. He filled two cups with coffee from the pot hanging on a metal bar over glowing embers in the fireplace and pulled a chair up facing Jill.

"Okay, shoot. Tell me what's wrong."

As Jill related to Tanner what Connie said, she watched his reactions closely. Sparks flew from his blue eyes, his jaw tightened and his hands clenched over his buckskin covered thighs. He stood suddenly, almost knocking over the chair, then began to pace the floor, his boot heels clicking in fast cadence on the wooden boards. His hand ran first over two week's growth of a new beard, then through his golden hair. He stopped dead in his tracks and turned steely eyes to Jill. "You believed her, didn't you?"

"I didn't want to, but..."

Tanner's eyes threw daggers at Jill as he interrupted, "You believed that woman? Even after I told you all the sneaky, conniving things she had done to get her way. Well, I guess that shows how much trust you have in me, doesn't it?" He turned on his heels and slammed out the door.

A repeat performance, Jill noted. When Tanner gets angry he just stomps away instead of talking things over. Maybe it would be just as well if she left now. She started to rise, then noticed a large piece of paper that had fallen under the table. She picked it up. It was a plan for an addition to Tanner's cabin. On the paper, the room in which she was now sitting became a living room; the front porch was closed in to become a kitchen and two additions were added to the other sides of the cabin. One contained a bedroom, bathroom and office. The other addition contained two more bedrooms, they were marked as *Alex* and *nursery*.

It was obvious Tanner did want children, but just as obvious that he planned on living with her when they were born. She'd been wrong to doubt him, wrong to have believed even a small part of what Connie said. She needed to apologize, and somehow regain his trust.

At the sound of the door opening, Jill looked up from the plans she held in her hand and was relieved to see a softer look on Tanner's face instead of the intense anger of a few moments ago.

"Truce? I didn't have a white flag, will this do?" Tanner handed her a two flower bouquet made out of a white paper napkin. One flower resembled a rose, the other a daisy, there were even leaves at the base of the stems.

Jill marveled at the intricacy of the bouquet. "Did you make this?"

Tanner looked embarrassed. "Yeah. Just a little something I picked up on a trip to Mexico."

"Where did you find the napkin?"

"Had it stuffed in my pocket."

"It's beautiful. I'm sorry for acting like such a fool. I love you so much I guess I just got scared." Jill gave Tanner a gigantic smile and moved into his arms.

He held her tightly, his chin moving on the top of her head as he talked. "I'm sorry too. I should have known Connie would pull some kind of a stunt and warned you. But as long as you don't believe what she said was true, it doesn't matter anymore. She'll never be able to come between us again."

"No, I won't let her, even if she tries again and again."

"She won't, Jill. That's part of the reason I was coming to the city tomorrow. Connie died."

Jill pushed back out of Tanner's arms and looked into his eyes, "She's dead?"

"Yes. Chet came yesterday to tell me that my father called. Connie had another heart attack. This time they couldn't save her. The funeral is tomorrow and I planned on being there, figured I owed her that much, but after what you just told me, I'm not going."

"But what about your parents? Won't they be upset if you don't attend?"

"Not anymore. Connie finally showed them her true colors when I was there last time." Something nicked at Tanner's conscience, stirring the feeling he wasn't handling this situation quite right. As a Christian, he was required to forgive, whether the person asked for it or not.

"But, I better go. It's not up to me to judge her. That's God's job."

Jill marveled at the way Tanner lived his beliefs. She wanted the kind of faith he had. "How do you do that? How can you so easily forgive someone who has hurt you?"

"It's not easy. And I can't do it on my own, but *I can do all things through Christ who strengthens me*."

"Is that another Bible verse?"

"Yes, it's Philippians 4:13. I found the verse when I was doing a word study on strength, something I felt I needed after losing both my brother and my wife. There are 41 verses that talk about God giving us strength, so it must be important to Him that we know He'll help us with it."

Tanner leaned down and held Jill's warm sweet lips in a long kiss. His breath ragged, his heart pounding, Tanner broke the kiss. His hands cupped her cheeks, while his lips dared to ask, "Will you marry me, Jill?" He took a deep breath and continued before letting Jill answer, "Wow, I didn't plan that, but, somehow, it just feels right. I don't have a ring to give you right now, but if you say yes, I'll get one when I come down the mountain.

CHAPTER 22

Jill accepted Tanner's proposal. They toasted their engagement with apple juice sipped from coffee mugs and ate a fancy celebration lunch of rabbit stew.

Tanner went outside to the shed for a few minutes and when he returned he reached into his pocket and withdrew a ring made of three strands of copper wire braided together. "Here, will this do until I get you a fancy ring?"

"Yes, put it on," Jill said as she held out her hand and waited until he finished slipping it on her finger.

"There, now, it's official," Tanner smiled and sealed the deal with a quick kiss.

Jill quickly caught on that her future husband was struggling with keeping their attraction under control. Not wanting to be the cause of him doing anything against his beliefs, she promptly changed the subject. "What is that thing you're building outside?"

"That thing…is a wind generator. It's going to supply you with electricity for your new home—I hope."

"You are a very creative person."

"Just wait, you ain't seen nothin' yet." Tanner got up from the table and went to the bookcase. He came back with the plans he had drawn up to pump water into the house. "There's a springhouse made of rocks half-buried in the ground outside. It looks like just a mound of dirt, or maybe a bomb shelter, and in the spring it gets so covered with ivy you can hardly see it."

Seeing by her frown that Jill didn't understand, Tanner went on, "A springhouse is built over or near a spring. Cold water runs through it to serve the same function as a refrigerator, only it's actually better because the air is not so compact. There is an air vent that measures about ten by twelve inches in the top of the springhouse that keeps the air circulating. The water enters from a holding trough through a four inch pipe and into another trough that is eighteen inches wide. Milk and butter are kept cool in that trough and there are shelves where canned fruits and vegetables are stored. I plan to tap into that water supply and pipe it directly in to the cabin, but we may still have to use the springhouse for keeping our food cold.

Jill was fascinated. "Sounds like you have everything figured out."

"Not quite. It still won't be the modern way you're used to living. Think you can handle that?"

"I think so." Jill smiled at Tanner, he seemed so unsure all of a sudden.

"And there aren't many people around. It's pretty quiet here, you may get lonely."

"I doubt it. I always wanted to live out in the country. I even tried several times to talk Tom into it, but he wanted no part of it. I like the peace and quiet, besides the whole Tuttle clan isn't too far away if I need entertainment. But what will we do about school for Alex?"

"Well, I have an idea. See what you think of this. We're going to build a church between Tuttle's place and ours."

"Who's building a church?"

"Some of the mountain people, and I'm helping. It seems they haven't had one here for a very long time. The last church got blown away in a big storm and they never bothered to rebuild because the minister left. Up here they call them a preacher."

"So do you have a new minister or preacher coming?

"I've been working with these mountaineers for a couple of years, trying to get them to understand they need the Savior. Something must have finally clicked because one of the young men has decided to pursue becoming a minister. He's down below going to Seminary and will be returning soon."

"What's all this stuff about a church got to do with school for Alex?"

"We figured we could utilize the building better by having it also be used as a school."

Jill wasn't sure about this plan. "How is Alex going to get there? It would be a long way for him to walk since it took us so long to get here from Tuttles."

"Things are changing up here. The State had decided it is time to connect the mountain people to the real world and they are going to be putting roads and bridges in that will make the distance much shorter. I think there is something else underfoot, but they're not telling what it is. Probably some new mining strike. Other kids from the area will be walking to school and Alex can go with them."

"Will a road come right past the cabin?"

"No."

"Then how am I going to be able to continue working with no road to the cabin?"

Tanner picked her up and twirled her around. "There will be one as soon as I can get the trail widened, darlin'."

All their problems, well, most of them anyway, were solved. Now all Jill had to do was sell her business, finish the houses she was working on, and plan a wedding. Plan a wedding! They hadn't even set a date. Panic began to strike.

"When do you want to get married?" she practically yelled at Tanner, she was so excited.

"Is tomorrow too soon?" he jokingly asked.

"Yes, of course. I'm serious. When?"

Tanner pulled Jill back into his arms. "I'll leave it up to you. But don't make me wait too long, Love. I need you with me."

Jill's mind whirled. "How about June?"

"June? But that's almost six months away," Tanner moaned.

"I know, but I have so much to do before we can get married. Will the church be built by then?"

"I doubt it, but the preacher will be here in a couple of months so we can use him instead of getting someone from down below. I don't want to spend time on building the church right now; I need to focus on our place first so you have a place to live. How about this? We can get married in June, you'd make a beautiful June bride, but if you sell your shop and get things lined up before that, could we move up the date?"

"I don't know. I'll have to think about it." Jill smiled teasingly at Tanner.

"Don't think too long, you might lose me. One of the Tuttle girls has been after me for a long time and it gets mighty lonely up here on all those cold winter nights."

Jill playfully punched his arm. "You are a big teaser, did you know that?"

Tanner stood and took Jill's hand, pulling her up with him. "So, are you ready to head over to Tuttle's and see if you can work a deal with them?'

"Yes, I am. It could be the solution to all my problems with that log house." They stood so close. When he was this near, Jill wanted to reach out and touch him, but memories of Tom not wanting to be touched kept her from reaching out to Tanner. Maybe someday the memories would go away. She hoped so; she didn't want them to mar her life with Tanner.

Conversation was what she needed to keep her mind and hands off this handsome man. "There is something I would like to know."

"Yes?" Tanner stood behind Jill. He wanted to reach out and touch her, pull her into his arms, but he sensed a distance she had silently put between them.

Jill was acutely aware of his closeness, but tried to keep the conversation light. "Why didn't you tell me about Chet's place when I was here before? You could have called someone to come and get me out of your hair right away."

Tanner laughed at Jill's subtle way of saying he had been keeping her there under false pretenses. He turned her around to face him. "Because Chet was gone then. Every year he takes off for his daughter's in Chattanooga. Sometimes he only spends a week, sometimes two. He claims it depends on how long he can stand the racket of six kids, two barking dogs and a son-in-law whose snores are more ear-splitting than a freight train's whistle when it loses its brakes going down the mountain."

Jill laughed, "My curiosity has gotten the best of me. How did he lose his ear?"

"Well, the story he told me was that some amorous young gal bit it off in a fit of passion. But W.H. says he was riding a wagon when they hit a rut in the frozen ground, Chet fell off and the metal wheel just sliced his ear clean off."

"Oh, that sounds awful." Jill's stomach turned queasy.

Tanner said, "It doesn't seem to bother Chet any. As a matter of fact, I think he enjoys all the attention he gets from it."

They finished their coffee and went to the Tuttles. At least this time Tanner didn't have to slow the mule down because of Jill's broken leg. Nor did they encounter any hungry mountain lions. The trip took a lot less time. Soon Jill was holding Maybelle's new baby girl, Sarah. Touching tiny fingers and little toes gave her an overwhelming desire to have another baby. She looked across the table at Tanner and could see his desire for a baby as well.

Jill laughed at the six children surrounding the table wanting her and Tanner's attention. She talked to Maybelle and Ned about her needs for the log house and possibly buying other things from their clan for future houses. They showed her their pottery and said the special pattern Jill's client wanted would be no problem to make. All her dreams about starting her specialized interior decorating business seemed to be coming true.

Maybelle brought out some of the quilts she'd made and some that had been done at "quiltin' bees" and explained the process of making them to Jill. The quilts were made by stuffing two to three pounds of wool between two pieces of muslin and adding a top made up of blocks sewn together. Patterns varied from the elaborate designs of the Poplar Leaf, each leaf set to point in the same direction or in groups of four to produce a four square pattern, to the simplicity of a string quilt made up of scraps of material pieced together anyway they fit.

One quilt especially caught Jill's eye. "This is beautiful. What is it called?" she asked as she held up the quilt. In the center was a white muslin heart. Fancy embroidery stitches attached the heart to a piece of red fabric and Maybelle and Ned's names were embroidered in the center of the heart. Surrounding it were smaller heart blocks made up of the same white hearts on red squares pattern. It looked like a very simple design, with the exception of all the fancy embroidery stitches and quilting designs of vines whose leaves where also hearts. Six of the small hearts had the names of their children Toby, Zeke, Annie, Tommie, Kathryn and Ben. Sarah's name had not yet appeared; apparently Maybelle hadn't had time to add it.

"Ain't got a name. Guess ya could call it a love quilt. I made it fer Ned after he asked me to marry 'im." Ned beamed at his wife and she at him. It was obvious they were still very much in love. "I added all the babies names when they were born. Haven't got around to adding Sarah's yet."

Tanner took Jill's hand in his. "Maybe Jill will learn how to make quilts and make one like that for me as a wedding present."

"A wedding present?" Maybelle and Ned stared at the pair across the table, then excitement filled the air as they talked of their plans for a summer wedding at Tanner's cabin.

CHAPTER 23

Jill returned to Knoxville to find a stack of mail and messages waiting at her shop. Her business was growing enough that she almost needed to hire another person, which should help it sell. She had no more than gotten started on the pile when Anna stepped into her office and told her there was a Brent and Nancy Baxter out in the showroom wanting to see her. She sighed, “Anna, you’ll have to tell them I just can’t take on any more jobs right now. I’m loaded with more than I can handle.”

“They aren’t here for that. They said something about wanting to get some advice on starting an interior decorating business of their own.”

Jill came to life. Could this be God’s answer to her prayer? No, couldn’t be. It didn’t seem like He had ever answered her prayers before. Why now? Regardless of whether it was God or not, she excitedly told Anna to show them into her office.

Brent Baxter was dark haired, very handsome and had a charming smile, while his wife, Nancy, had long coppery-colored hair and a cute pertness. They explained that Nancy was an interior decorator working for one of Jill's competitors and Brent was an accountant for a law firm. Both good jobs, but they decided to go into business for themselves.

When Jill told them she wanted to sell hers but still be able to work out of it when she was in the city, they were ecstatic. She would finish up the jobs she had taken by the middle of May, train the Baxters, and have two weeks to pack and put the finishing touches on her wedding. It was the perfect solution for everyone, including Anna, who would be kept on the job.

A week later an agreement was signed between Jill and the Baxters for the purchase of the decorating business, contingent upon them getting the loan. The Baxters would act as managers until all the paperwork was finalized. With the Baxters in charge, Jill could concentrate on concluding the jobs she had scheduled. She was taking a month off after the wedding, then back to work.

Happy was too small a word for what she was feeling. Everything was falling into place perfectly. Maybe Tanner was right, God was a detail man, wanting to be involved in even the smallest parts of her life. She was definitely thinking more about God. Each morning He seemed to pop into her mind. She wasn't very good at prayers, but would end up with a short one-sided conversation with God at the start of her day. Maybe that was why things seemed to be going so much better—God really was listening.

Alex would no longer need a sitter. Tanner wanted to take care of him when she was working. In another week Tanner would be in the city for a couple of days so she could meet his family. Nervousness assailed her just thinking about it.

It was as if that nervousness beckoned Dr. Samuel Tanner to her door. He arrived one evening when Jill was studying pictures of wedding dresses.

After entering the living room, even before sitting down, Dr. Tannner said, “My son tells me the two of you are getting married in June. Up on that confounded mountain, of all places.”

“Yes,” Jill answered quietly.

“Why? He needs to be here taking over my practice, not up there messing around with some herbs.”

“I don’t think…”

“You don’t need to think about anything, you need to convince him to come back. I want him here. This is where he belongs. My clinics are making a lot of money, but they would make a lot more if he were to join me again.”

He glanced at her when he was finished speaking, apparently hoping the word money would have some effect.

Jill’s hands stopped fidgeting, amazed at what she had just heard. She looked into the eyes of a man who didn’t resemble Tanner at all. He had a strong, pointed chin and long, pointed nose. Her first thought was that they stuck out so he could put them in other people’s business, namely hers and Tanner’s. But she told herself that wasn’t fair; she really didn’t know the man. So she decided to try and make him understand a little better.

Her voice was steady, “Look, Dr. Tanner…”

“Sam, please.”

Now it seemed as if Sam was going to try a more friendly approach, “Look, Sam, I cannot, nor will I, try to convince Tanner to come back to your practice. He knows what he wants to do and I fully support him. What he is trying to accomplish, what he will accomplish, is for the benefit of a world of people, not just a few who can afford medicine. One day, in the not too distant future, I’m sure, both you and I will be very proud of what he has been able to accomplish.”

“Humph. I could be proud of what he does here just as well.” Sam stood, walked to the door, opened it and said, “I won't trouble you anymore. I can see you're not willing to help me, so I'll have to find another way. I expect you'll keep this conversation between us?" After Jill agreed, he left, shutting the door firmly behind him.

~~~~~~~~

Tanner arrived a week later and picked her up to go meet his parents. Jill wanted to tell him about her visit with his father, but she had made a promise and planned to keep it.

When they arrived at Tanner's parent's home, Sam opened the door, appearing to be a little nervous when Tanner introduced them. Jill figured it was because he was pretending to have never met her. She smiled, reached out her hand and said, "Thank you for inviting me into your home." Being around Tanner had taught her not to lie, no matter what, so that was all she could think of to say.

Tanner's mother stood beside her husband, but instead of holding out her hand, she hugged Jill and ruffled Alex's hair. "Hi, I'm Sadie and I am so glad to meet both of you. I haven't seen my son so happy in a long time."

Sadie ushered them into a large living room. Logs burning in the fireplace gave the room a warm glow. The home was nicely decorated in a simple country style. Pictures of Tanner, his brother Tim and the grandchildren were scattered about the room. Jill had to admit she was surprised that with their wealth, they didn't have a much fancier home.

Tanner'sister-in-law, Gail, was seated near the fireplace on one of the sofas. At a table in a corner of the room, three children were playing a card game. Tanner pulled Gail out of her chair and into a hug. "Come on, Gail. Let's introduce Jill and Alex to your little band of hooligans." He took Alex's hand and led
~~~~~~~~

him over to the table; Gail and Jill followed. "Alex, I want you to meet your new cousins—Seth, Billy and Abby. Seth is the oldest, he's 11. Even though Billy is almost as tall as Seth, he's only nine. And this little seven-year-old munchkin," Tanner pulled her ponytail, "is Abby."

Abby giggled and asked, "Do you want to play Uno with us? I'll help you." They left Alex in the care of Gail's children and turned to rejoin the adults.

"I need to go check on dinner," Sadie said."I'll be back in a little bit. Gail, will you help me?"

They hadn't been gone long when Sam turned to Tanner, "Son, why don't you go and see if your mother needs a hand. If nothing else, visit with her a little. She misses you an awful lot. Besides, I want a chance to get to know my future daughter-in-law a little better."

After Tanner left the room, Sam didn't say anything for a long time. Jill dreaded what was coming.

"You know, Jill, I think you and Sadie are right. I shouldn't interfere in David's life. I also think you're the kind of woman who will stand by and work with her husband, just like my Sadie has all these years. I started out with only a small office and one examining room many years ago. Now I own three clinics and am on the board of directors at the hospital. I would have bought Sadie a fully-staffed mansion, but she refused to move from this home, the one we purchased early in my career and where we raised our sons.

"When I started pressuring David, I forgot how important it is to make your own mark on the world; to feel as if what you are doing will make a difference in the lives of others. I'm sure you will make my son very happy. If you don't mind, I would like to keep our previous little talk just between us. Sadie would be so angry if she found I asked you to help me pressure David into coming back. She's been telling me for years to leave the boy alone and let him do what he wants," he chuckled. "She was right, as usual."

After dinner, Alex played happily with the children while the adults discussed the Tanner and Morgan wedding plans. Jill especially liked Sadie. She guessed it was because she and Tanner were so much alike, both blonde and blue eyed with the same temperament—quick to bluster and just as quick to mellow.

~~~~~~~~

Tanner made the trip into the city every two weeks to see her. He wouldn't let her come back to the mountain until it was time for their wedding, claiming he wanted everything finished before she saw it. The time sped by and on the last day of May, Jill and Alex, Carrie and her two boys and Jack all went up the mountain to stay at Tanner's cabin until the wedding the next day. Tanner was staying at the Tuttle's.

The first day of June dawned bright and sunny. Jill stood in slip and stockings looking out the window of the bedroom she and Tanner would soon share. Sunlight shone on profusely colored flowerbeds. The perfect blooms of the orange-red and cream bicolored roses called Eternity would be a part of her bouquet, as would the classic white Calla Lilies. Airy wisps of Baby's Breath were being fastened into her upswept hair by Carrie's deft hands. As Carrie tucked in the last of the flowers, she said, "There, all done. Now we'd better get into our dresses or you'll be late for your own wedding."

"I better check on Alex first."

Carrie grabbed Jill's arm to keep her from leaving the room.
~~~~~~~~

"He's fine. Jack is taking care of getting the boys ready. Are you just trying to kill time because you're nervous, or what?"

"I'm not nervous. I have done this before, you know."

"Oh, yeah? Then how come you're biting your bottom lip like you always do when you're nervous?"

Jill let the soft skin caught between her teeth slide out slowly and admitted. "Well, maybe I am, just a little. Everything has happened so fast since I met Tanner. I guess I'm a little scared."

"Of what?"

"Of wild animals in the woods."

"Tanner has a gun."

"Of not having a phone."

"There's one not two miles away."

"Of not being a good wife." Two tiny tears slipped from Jill's eyes.

Carrie put her arms around her friend. "Not to worry. You'll be fine. You've just got those pre-marriage jitters that everyone gets. Now, let me help you."

Since both she and Tanner had been married once before, Jill chose a simple cream-colored sheath. She lifted the golden heart locket out of its blue velvet box and watched as sunlight sparkled off the diamonds before hooking it around her neck. She stretched her left hand out before her and once again admired the marquise-cut diamond engagement ring Tanner had given her the night she met his family. Soon it would be interlocked with its matching wedding band, legally connecting her heart to Tanner's.

The ceremony was held outside Tanner's newly remodeled cabin on the beautifully verdant mountainside. The rich scent of wild flowers, such as rhododendron and honeysuckle, wafted through the air. Mockingbirds and robins sang in perfect harmony as Jill and Tanner were joined together as man and wife.

The picnic style lunch was served by the Tuttle clan's women. Jill warned everyone beforehand *not* to ask what they were eating, just to eat it. But Maybelle surprised her by ordering some of their precious chickens to be butchered and served for this special occasion.

At Tanner's request, the moonshine jug was left behind, but that didn't stop the music from happening. W.H. picked the strings of his banjo, while Chet played the fiddle. Everyone joined in singing some songs Jill had never heard and others she remembered hearing, like *Cripple Creek, Springfield Mountain* and *Casey Jones.* Jill and Tanner sat with their hands locked together and watched the high stepping and twirling to the square dance music being played, that is, until Maybelle and Ned pulled them in to join the dance.

Just before dusk the visitors left and the Tuttle clan packed up everything and headed home. Maybelle and Ned took Alex with them so the newlyweds could have the night to themselves. Soon everyone was gone.

Jill and Tanner sat outside for a little longer watching the glowing sun disappear behind the rounded peaks of the mountains. Tanner edged his fingers along Jill's cheek, tilting her chin up and sprinkling feather light kisses all over her face as he murmured into her ear, "Think we should go in, Love?"

Jill nodded her assent and playfully nuzzled the soft beard attempting to grow back to its former glory. She ran her hand down his already shoulder length hair as he scooped her up in his arms, carried her into the cabin and set her on the bed.

"Tanner, I have a present for you."

"And I have one for you. Do you want to go first or should I?"

Jill watched Tanner shift from one foot to the other. He was obviously nervous about giving her the gift. Maybe it wasn't very nice but she was going to make him wait. She couldn't wait to see his reaction. "I'll go first." She jumped off the bed, opened the doors of the large closet Tanner had built in their new bedroom and pulled a red and white heart-patterned quilt off the shelf. She handed the quilt to Tanner. "I'm afraid I have to admit Maybelle did most of the sewing on this, but I did enjoy it enough to want to pursue learning how to quilt."

Tanner ran his hands over the soft fabric. "It's beautiful. Thank you." He grinned like a little boy getting caught stealing from the cookie jar. "Now, it's my turn. Yesterday, I got a contract in the mail from Sorkey Publishing for a book on herbal remedies."

"Oh, Tanner, that's great. Just what you wanted. But how did they know about your research and how come you didn't tell me about this before now?" She playfully punched Tanner's arm.

"I wasn't sure if it would happen. About six months ago, I wrote them a letter telling a little bit about the research and its results, suggesting that a book may help in foreign countries where medical help is not available. They could be given away with Bibles by missionaries working in some of the poorer countries. I received a letter back from a Mr. Tony Sorkey telling me they thought it was a wonderful idea, but where was the money going to come from to help pay for the printing and shipping of the books? Sorkey informed me they did donate to charities; however they were not in the business of giving away all their money. Until I could come up with a plan for them to make a modest profit, they were not interested in my book."

Jill frowned, "Wait, I thought you said you got a contract for the book. I'm confused."

"I know, but it just goes to show how God works in mysterious ways." Tanner lifted a letter off the dresser. "Here read this, then you'll understand."

Jill read out loud, "Dear Dr. Tanner, I apologize for my son's earlier letter. In his zeal to show a healthy bottom line, I'm afraid he has forgotten God's rules are different than the ordinary businessman's and are much more successful. I'm sure you are familiar with it, but just as a healthy reminder here is one of God's very profitable rules, not only financially, but spiritually as well. Luke 6:38—'Give and it will be given to you: good measure, pressed down, shaken together, and running over will be put into your bosom. For with the same measure that you use, it will be measured back to you.'

"Please accept this contract with the understanding that we at Sorkey Publishing will stand the total cost of printing and shipping the book. You, however, must make arrangements for where they are to be sent. May God's blessings be upon you, William Sorkey."

While Jill sat stunned by the letter she had just finished reading, Tanner reached under the bed and drew out a box covered in gilded silver wrap, tied with red ribbon and topped with a multitude of red bows and curly ribbon streamers. "Here, I have another present."

Jill carefully removed the ribbons and paper, opened the box and gasped as she removed a telephone. "What…?"

"I thought if you were going to be working from home you might need that. The phone company will be stringing wire from Chet's to here sometime in the next couple of weeks." He took Jill in his arms and looked deep into the eyes that reminded him of warm hot fudge. "You've made me the happiest man in the whole world, Love. I have you, and Alex. What more could a man ask for?"

LaVergne, TN USA
09 March 2011
219341LV00001B/37/P

9 781456 011871